GEORGE BOWERING

George Bowering is a distinguished novelist, poet, editor, professor, historian and tireless supporter of fellow writers. Bowering has authored more than one hundred books and chapbooks, including works of poetry, fiction, autobiography, biography and fiction for young readers. His writing has been translated into French, Spanish, Italian, German, Chinese and Romanian. His novel, *Burning Water,* won the Governor General's award for fiction and his memoir, *Pinboy*, was shortlisted for the BC National Award for non-fiction in 2013. In 2002, Bowering was recognized by the *Vancouver Sun* as one of the most influential people in British Columbia.

Anvil Press's Lost BC Literature Series

The Anvil Press "Lost BC Literature Series" was established to bring important out-of-print BC literature to a new audience of readers. Other titles in the "Lost BC Literature" series include *Who Killed Janet Smith?* by Ed Starkins (originally published in 1984), *A Credit to Your Race* by Truman Green (originally published in 1973), and *Some Girls Do*, Teresa McWhirter's debut novel (originally published in 2002) *Mirror on the Floor* was originally published by McClelland and Stewart in 1967.

a Novel by
George Bowering

ANVIL PRESS | 2014

Copyright © 1967, 2014 by George Bowering

All rights reserved. No part of this book may be reproduced by any means without the prior written permission of the publisher, with the exception of brief passages in reviews. Any request for photocopying or other reprographic copying of this book must be directed in writing to access: The Canadian Copyright Licensing Agency, One Yonge Street, Suite 800, Toronto, Ontario, Canada, M5E 1E5.

Anvil Press Publishers Inc.
P.O. Box 3008, Main Post Office
Vancouver, B.C. V6B 3X5 CANADA
www.anvilpress.com

Library and Archives Canada Cataloguing in Publication

    Bowering, George, 1935-, author
        Mirror on the floor : a novel / by George Bowering.

(Lost BC lit)
Originally published: Toronto : McClelland and Stewart
    Limited, 1967.

ISBN 978-1-927380-95-6 (pbk.)

    I. Title.

PS8503.O875M57 2014   C813'.54   C2014-900726-4

Lost BC Lit Series
Cover design by Dave Barnes
Interior by HeimatHouse

Represented in Canada by Publishers Group Canada
Distributed in Canada by Raincoast Books and in the US by SPD (Berkeley)

The publisher gratefully acknowledges the financial assistance of the Canada Council for the Arts, the Canada Book Fund, and the Province of British Columbia through the B.C. Arts Council and the Book Publishing Tax Credit.

Chapter Seventeen of this book was published originally in *Queen's Quarterly*.

PRINTED AND BOUND IN CANADA

THIS BOOK IS DEDICATED TO BILL TRUMP

FOREWORD

Mirror on the Floor [1967] is George Bowering's first published novel, a precursor in a distinguished and prolific literary career. Well received in its day, *Mirror* retains its brilliance after almost half a century, bringing to light, and to life, a particular context that is all but forgotten today. This is Vancouver of fifty years ago, a provincial port city of wooden buildings and antique liquor laws, of tobacco smoke and tethered telephones, of cars without seat belts and college boys without enough sense to stay out of trouble.

Bob, the narrator, is a university student who is in love with language and excited by the exotic allure of the big city. One night, out with his pal exploring the seedier side of town, things turn ugly. However, morning offers compensation in the form of a chance encounter with an intriguing young woman, whose dysfunctions seem only to enhance her attractiveness. As their troubled relationship spins out of control, Bob tries to step back, asserting that he is not responsible. The world just happens, he says, and he gets along by throwing words at it, telling his story the way it is, as his sentences tumble onto the page, fully packed, bursting with descriptors, charged with youthful exuberance and the energy of his own personal obsessions.

As you read this novel, notice how the idiom has changed since that time, how Bob uses words like "girl," "Miss," "Lady," "negro,"

"Indian," etc, terms which have since sunk into disuse and disrepute under the weight of their own accumulated connotations. This is part of the experience. A contemporary reader tastes a world that is no longer with us. Those words, sounds, shapes, smells, textures—take them. This is a little chunk of history: Vancouver on the cusp of the '60s. If I had to choose a single word to characterize *Mirror*, I would say "authentic." Bowering was there. So was I.

—Lionel Kearns, May 2014

CHAPTER ONE

I DON'T KNOW HOW we happened to be there, Delsing and me sitting at a table with a little old ex-seaman psychoanalyzing us and occasionally going into a mewing tirade against them dirty union finaglers and every once in a while gesturing slapstick style toward a big bottle bulge in the pocket of his sad hanging blue overcoat. Though as I cast back my ruminating mind I remember a rip-rapping ride down the long streets of Vancouver towards the Main Street gorge, my poor old over-travelled yellow Morris Minor sniffing happily at the prospect of a race, like some old horse on a junkwagon smelling water after a dizzying day in the hot sun of back alleys junk ride, the feeble yellow radio crackling static along with the crazy Mexican maraca music I love so well, *ay ay ay ay ahi,* only reminder now of that unbelievable and near-fatal summer I spent in old Xalapa doing things just like this, but not quite, not in the dismal winter rain of Main Street Vancouver winter, Delsing and me sitting in a beer-parlour across the street from Mickey Chang's notorious morphine café.

But there we were, and there he was, telling us of him a young man lost three fingers from his left hand, bitten by a mad drunk fellaheen native on the brown shore of Borneo in thirty-six when the union was on your side boy and not a bunch of whiteshirt dandies looking for a breast pocket full of cigars and a new shirt every two days. He was funny-looking in his blue coat and white turtleneck sweater, funny that's all. Surprising thing, to me anyway—Delsing was looking over his shoulder every thirty seconds at the hockey game on the TV high on the wall—was that he had all his teeth in the front anyway, something I don't look for in this end of the stinking water street. But of course they were false, with the expected possession-pride in the strangest things you always should expect to find here or anywhere where a man has to believe in anything that doesn't fit in his derelict mind, like a Japanese transistor hearing-aid or a gold nugget ring, which I have seen too, and got over my momentary surprise.

"What you got there, Barney?" I said at last, because it wasn't Barney of course, but he thought if he had to tell us a name he would expect us, being outsiders, to really imagine that Barney was a natural name for Main Street, because it was the kind of name you find in Jiggs comic strips and Jackie Gleason TV shows, and just because both were way beyond his comfortable reach and interest, he expected in his poor proud mind that we would be delightedly convinced.

"Come in the can." And I have heard that before, a lot of times, but I'm a foot taller than he was and so of course I went, because I have a predilection for wine and of course that was what he had. Not drinking wine. Soliciting wine. Eighty-seven cents.

So in the washroom, evil-smelling labyrinth down the row of tables out two sick green doors in the back, into the maroon-painted room of chipped and cracked white in places crooked imitation tile walls, cigarette butts in the brown soggy swirl on the floor under the devices, I received the object from him and tore off the roll of liquor-store brown paper, twisted off the cap and tilted the cheap green bottle to my now salivating mouth, and glugged down a generous grapy several mouthfuls of the wine, returning the bottle after he had gestured the old again, twice.

He struggled the bottle back into his coat pocket, and I started for the door, but he said, "Uhhh..." and it was the practised grabbing voice method of the expert and subtle panhandler. But he was no panhandler, at least not tonight—he had those front teeth, and another thing, his face and chin were shaven clean, a kind of clean that says something is wrong, out of place, and be careful. So I slowed down and just shuffled, as if starting politely the two of us out the door, waiting for him politely, but he started to talk.

"I hope you don't mind me saying so, but your friend, he could get in trouble, you know? I mean he looks kind of like a smart guy, just looking around to see if he can see anything funny. Now you, I can tell you're different. You ever been to sea?"

"No." I had, a little, but I had my reasons for hushing now.

"You could have fooled me, and I'm not easy to fool, not old Frank Levine."

Finally I got him going out to the table again, and Delsing was sitting there, pouring our beer into his glass. He still had that expression on his face, the one Barney had picked out, though as a spring for another reason that he was too nervous or too sober to really set in action, and the old guy passed Delsing the bottle under the table, and Delsing toddled as if he really had to take a hell of a piss out back to the smelly can, and I ordered more beer, though I was onto the wine now and wished I had a whole bottle of it, feeling a little guilty because not drunk enough yet, but wishing I could con Barney/Frankie out of the quart, though I felt a little justified because of what I suspected—but that's all, maybe I was wrong, maybe I should have been indifferent like Delsing who has I imagine been sheltered against that sort of thing, except maybe in the high-school washroom and once or twice in the air force, if he was really in it as he claims.

"Yep, your friend is a quiet one, but not because he's smart. You're the smart one, aren't you Robbie?" I'd told him my name was Robbie, and I guess it is, but I usually go by another one. I told him Delsing's name was Neatly, but Delsing said no it ain't, it's Delsing and I don't give a shit who knows it, and that's what the guy probably didn't believe.

"He *must* be smart, I don't see him coming back with your wine," I said, though I can imagine him in the evil washroom, taking for form and romantic night on skid row a little tongue in-the-way sip and putting the cap on the bottle and maybe trying to do something in the urinal. But I was wrong, because when I got the bottle there was a good two inches gone, and Delsing just quietly sitting there again, looking over his shoulder at the Montreal Canadiens beating somebody five to nothing.

"Ah that's all right all right, I never drink it, just have it for my friends," said Barney in the can again, as I tried to get ahead of Delsing who was winning the contest all around, probably out there now drinking all our beer, waiting for us to come back so he can take another fake leak while I'm buying the round again, no question of Barney buying it.

And pretty soon it was gone, and we were all sitting there, trying to order more beer before the bar closed for midnight, and once again Barney was telling us how he knew Delsing was a college student and I was a friend who had to work for a living probably longshoring because of my hat. "I'm sort of a natural-born amateur psychologist," he said. And Delsing, who has been going with that girl in the psych department, snorted loudly and beerily, and that made Barney not only more hostile toward him, but stronger in his machinations to ensure that I was a real good friend that he could see as soon as he saw me, and I told him sure he could sit with us and chased away the waiter for beer when he moved our way silently offering his services if we were being bothered by a man who must be a chronic neighbourhood bother and potential trouble-maker and eliminator of customers.

So that when the place closed, and a good time after, when we emerged from the old wooden hotel, we were all together, me wondering how Barney was going to imagine a way to get rid of Delsing or whether it would be worth the risk or whether it would be necessary.

"I simply must have more of that delicious wine, Barney, and it being Saturday night the stores are closed, and you said you knew a place," I said, counting my money with my hand rummaging with mysterious soft paper and coins in my pocket. Where it went later I don't know.

"Not yet, man. Not for half an hour yet, then we'll be off and running," said the little man with an uncomforting slur in his voice.

So we went over to Mickey Chang's café across the dark street, into the hot smoky turbulence that hung there every night after the pubs were closed off.

"Well, what do you think?" I said, plunging head-first into the angry smoky dead end of the night room.

Distracted and wily Delsing: "I think *Moby-Dick* is one whale of a book"—and he mused in after us, following us as if placing his trust that we would find him a seat and maybe push him into it and materialize a cup of Chang coffee, wretched milk-laden stuff, on the table under his propped-up head. And that way we got a booth, miraculously, in the squash of Saturday night bodies—junkies, hookers, alkies, rubbies, guys maybe just an hour away from dying in an alley up against a garbage can or on a gray-stripe mattress in a brown-red hotel up on the fifth floor above an empty parking lot. Coffee in front of us, Delsing propping his head and looking at the coffee, saying probably I'm going to come down there and drink you you son of a bitch.

Mickey Chang's is the last place; you come there when you're eighteen years old and in Vancouver for the first time and you probably get away, or you come there when you're an old man forty-five years and no chance of dying more than four blocks from the place with the dirty red neon rooster hanging crooked over the door, waiting to fall on a head and kill someone, anyone. Pinball machines banging away up front around the door into the night or maybe the sea. Counter seats full of guys making coffee last hours and other guys trying to cadge three pennies to make up the dime, old guys with dead rolled cigarette butts in their mouths, brown spittle hanging out the corner of the mouth down on white-gray beard, matted-up trails of whiskers. Young Swedes with brawny uncontrolled arms around the pink sweater shoulders of slightly fat Coast Indian girls, trying to set up an all night situation they don't know where, nobody's got hold of a car tonight. Now I'm trying to remember where my car is, wondering if it's all right or maybe there's three guys in tight greasy garage jeans working on the no-draft windows with long pieces of wire. Mickey Chang, fat Chinese, scared and crafty behind the bar, watchful to stop fights and situations before the cops come again tonight, last night they stomped in and pulled two guys out of the dingy can with no lock (men or women or both) and had a screening at the door, looking for forty caps of reported heroin and maybe getting in a few unsatisfying feels. Old Dorothy there tonight as every night, telling about her convent days in England and singing happy horny songs and jigging around with her hands under her awesome sagging breasts, bouncing them up and down, old woman maybe between fifty and sixty drinking coffee at every table and calling Mickey Chang a run of dirty race names. Gang of Indian kids in tee-shirts at the back, standing by a booth, long shiny black hair combed and eased back, dark eyes looking for an insult from some drunk. Rag ends of people sitting in all the booths with empty cups and old chow mein plates with cigar ashes and balled napkins all over the place.

"You sure you can get the wine, Frankie?" I said.

"I can get it, I know the place. Two fifty, but not for fifteen minutes yet."

He was looking at the door, him getting smaller all the time, hunching there across from Dels and me against the oniony green booth. He had his coat yanked up around him as if it was a cold night on the ocean. He took his eyes off the door and jammed a nickel with bits of pocket tobacco all over it into the little machine on the wall. Pretty soon some blurry saxophone chant droned through the room and the crazy noises of the people around.

"I'll be right back, just stay, I'm going to the can, I'll just be a minute. Don't go away, eh?"—looking at me from his half-out-of-the-seat position.

"We'll be here."

"Till the cows go home," said Delsing.

"Come on, Delsing, you got to be digging everything all the time, and there's more wine, wine all over the city, how can you sit there not bothering to dig everything?" I said, and I got that funny burping feeling in the back of my throat.

He just sat there picking pieces of tobacco off the mouth-end of his cigarette, picking them out, dropping them on the wet of the table, And the two new guys said mind if we sit here and share the booth and we said okay or at least I did, Delsing just brooded with eyes must have been purple he looked like Miles Davis frowning down painfully and haughty over the whole world from the top of a three-rung stool. One of the guys was an Indian, probably an unemployed logger, looking as if he had walked on his hands all his life pushing his face into the rough ground, he had so many old crooked scars and a flat nose mushed up so the nostrils stuck out to the side in little hairy triangles. He was sullen, with his neck pulled down into the top of an old army high-collar sweater covered with stains like old stepped-on coffee puddles. The other guy was big in the kind of way that made you think of a sorry big animal stuck for the rest of his life in the zoo. He was bald and he had suntan and freckles on the scalp stretched tight over the top of his big bony head. There was an unbelievably little straight pipe with a speck of tobacco or something burning red in it, pointing out the side of his whiskery mouth. One of those things you expect like I said to see there down where the wash of the sea meets the scraping piles of the land.

"Buy ya a coffee?" I said, and they shouted to the nearest old Chinese with a soppy apron hanging under his belly.

And it came, soupish-looking stuff the dull yellowy-grey colour of a pair of socks I once wore for three weeks in a row, tasted a little different, not much. The two new guys moved over it hunched like a couple of plainsmen caught in the beginnings of a storm, but really out of habit, not letting anyone who might be anyone at all see what you've got. The Indian was looking all around, casing the place constantly, a bird. The other guy just sat there, little pipe in mouth, and looked way down into his cup of whatever it really was, as if the liquid contained all the whorl of the cosmos.

"How's it going," I ventured, and they gruffed a few all rights same as usuals.

Then the Indian pulled his neck in and got loquacious all of a sudden. "Rotten night, eh, Murray, just like the night Elsie got killed. You guys never seen Elsie that's my wife got killed in a fight with a bunch of guys knife right in the neck. She was a good woman, Elsie. Wasn't she, Murray? Murray knew her, never was a better woman, except once in a while she got on the stuff."

It went through my mind: were these guys trying to con a couple of ingenues?

"That's right. That's right," said the big guy. Murray.

And me wondering where's Barney, because he was supposed to be just gone to the can and it was just punched in the back wall a few yards away, and I'd seen other people, I guess they were, going in there where there shouldn't have been room for one guy standing back far enough to miss his pant legs.

So I said I had to go heh heh and squeezed my way into the can where he was alone all right and he grabbed my arm which I didn't shake off because there wasn't enough room, and he looked at me as if I had stood him up or something.

"Don't mess around with those guys, they're no good business you shouldn't have bought them a coffee. Especially your friend. I told you he would be in trouble, and the best thing for you to do is get out of here with me and leave him with them, because you're going to get yourself in deep. Those guys don't just fool around. Come on, eh, let's get ourselves a bottle of wine, you and me."

All the time looking kind of desperate, and I understood kind of, because he had seen us first so to speak, and he was losing the fish just before he got it ashore, and it was dangerous in some mysterious way. What was the matter with those guys out there I wanted to know.

"Never mind," he said, "the less you know about them the better, especially the Indian. I've known those guys a long time and you haven't, so I can tell you it's no good."

I told him sorry I couldn't just leave Delsing there no matter what and why didn't he just come and sit with the lot of us and we'd get rid of the two guys pretty soon. But when I came out again he went over and sat at the end of the counter not too close to our rickety old booth.

I could tell when I came back that things hadn't got any smoother between the two guys and Delsing, whatever was the matter with Dels, because the Indian was looking mean at him and the big guy putting his arm out on his friend and soothing him. Sorta looking hard into Delsing's forehead and leaning forward off his seat, all the time his silent friend's hard arm on his chest up high, the Indian was saying, "She was a good woman, my wife, only sixteen when I married her and nineteen when she died, she was a good woman, my wife, eh, Murray? Cops. My wife she was and I had to sit in a fuckin hole for six months when the cops came around they never bother coming around when your wife is alive. Why don't you drink your coffee?"

Delsing: "Yeah, coffee, it's not so hot, is it?"

"You a cop?"

"Nooh." Delsing's voice went up on the second syllable, the little sneaking-in of the hurt boy not able to explain jazz he pulls when he wants you to think he's innocent and can't understand what you're talking about. Of course at first I didn't believe the Indian could think Delsing was a cop, I thought he was just trying to be aggressive thinking Delsing was chicken, but then not a second later I knew that's what he all of a sudden did think, and I was worried that Delsing was going to get us both in fist-hammering trouble before we would get out of Mickey Chang's.

"You're acting like a cop, fella, if you're a cop you're going to get trouble tonight and I don't care what you and your fuckin friends think you can do about it."

"Well, I ain't a cop," says Delsing, as if he was J. Edgar Hoover.

I was starting to plot hypotenuses and arcs figuring out the shortest safe distance to the door past the guys that all seemed to be starting to edge in their ears and quiet faces to what was going on in our booth. But Murray managed to keep the Indian in his seat for now anyway, and I noticed old Frank sitting at the counter with a cup of the slopping coffee in his hand, grinning a wily little grin on one side of his mouth. I could see the morning rainstreet Vancouver papers: COLLEGE STUDENTS KILLED IN MAIN STREET MASSACRE. Epitaph for George Delsing and Bob Small. I wanted out of there and back in my little tin car.

But Delsing was the way he had always been in a thing like this—scared I knew and wanting to get out of there, but also fascinated or proud or gleaming gratified in his own image, not wanting to move, wanting to sit there in the tension waiting to see just what *was* going to happen. He always used to be like that, climbing tough mountains and making me jealous because of all the risks he took and taking them I think mostly because he knew I wasn't going to. I couldn't find out if he was scared or just crazy experiencing. "Experiencing, Small, ole Buddy, that's what it's all about," he always said, and I didn't always like it.

"Nice watch you got, cop," said the Indian, not nicely.

Because that was right, there wouldn't be anybody in that smoky yellow-coffee place with a shiny watch on his skinny arm on a Saturday night. And I think Delsing had slipped it down from inside his sleeve where he had put it before coming into the place.

"I already told you—"

"You already told me."

I thought it was time I said something, little as I wanted to, partly because I told myself the conversation seemed to be tailing out, and partly because I wanted to take the attention off my friend who was not exactly exerting himself to avoid a slambang smashing of the head bones. I was grooming myself for the diplomatic corps, anyway, I mean really, in college.

"You're worried I guess cause he bought you a cup of coffee like a maybe FBI investigator fink," I said. And then I didn't go on for various reasons, one of them being that there wasn't anything I was ready to say.

"Never mind," said Delsing, and he started to get up and squat along out of the booth that was slipping and swaying like everything else in the place.

And I was glad nobody tried to stop him or annoy him, because I think he would have smashed his head right into a fight, if not to settle things, at least to get it over with and get rid of the annoying bother of this not knowing if he was going to get it or not. But it worked out worse than that.

Because there was a sudden quiet in the place, and when I looked around I saw everyone was sitting still like the very end of a dance scene in a movie musical, and all looking hard at what they were doing, and nobody was talking except one guy way at the back, whose lone voice carried out embarrassing loud all over the café, and he stopped short when he noticed this too.

The front of the café was aswarm with big cops, bigger than they probably were, because they were wearing their heavy blue-black winter coats and they were situating themselves like in a bad movie, but you knew they were used to this, it wasn't just a set stage, it was the efficient way to get ready all right.

And Delsing I guess didn't notice till too late, till he was all wound up going out the door, getting out in the street away from all the tension, and when he got stopped it was not by any Indian or fawning old Frank, it was by the belly of a cop, and before he knew what it was he'd run up against, Delsing was peevishly trying to push his way past, and he was grabbed, not gently. I was up and out of my seat, wobbling around, forgetting all about the other guys, getting to the front, when I saw Delsing, still peevy, still not knowing, trying to pull his arm away from the big cop's hand and get going out the door, and I saw the cop slam him up against a wall. I was worried then, but Delsing suddenly I guess noticed what was going on, and he stood really still. I was a little afraid he would lip up, but he didn't. Not then.

But I guess I didn't show enough reserve myself. A few seconds and I was up against the cop shouting let him go, he was just thinking of something else, he didn't even know you guys were here, I want to explain all this.

And the cop that was holding limp Delsing up by the armpit said, "You just relax, just get back there and relax, buddy."

The beer and wine in me, I guess, it was something coming up inside, anyway, and when it reached my throat it was words. "Look, whaddya think, he's a dope fiend or something? I'm trying to tell you something, trying to avert a misunderstanding, I'm trying to help, do you understand? Can you grasp it, I'm attempting to prevent a miscarriage of justice!"

"Okay, that's it, buddy," said another cop voice, and I was grabbed from behind and pushed up against a wall. Cop procedure.

"Hands against the wall!"

"Spread your legs!"

There were hands running up my legs, around my ribs and into my armpits. I saw another cop was doing the same to sullen down-staring Delsing. Guys were being lined up all over the place, and cop hands were running all over them. From the back of the room I heard a little scuffle and a meaty thump.

"You son of a whore," someone said in a sore-throated kind of whisper.

So that's what it was after all, a narcotics raid. In the paper a few days before there had been a story about a guy choked dead by a constable looking for swallowed capsules. Line of duty. I was relieved even in the moment of outrage anti-gestapo drunken Main Street unbelievable dream, and I was just so glad it wasn't me I saw them dragging out of the café with blood and torn little scraps of mouth all over his face.

"Okay, what's your name, let's see your identification," said my cop.

I pulled out my fat old wallet and he took it from me, looking in all the pockets and coming out with a green and white card, my birth certificate.

"Name?"

"As it says on there, Robert Small."

"Age?"

"Twenty-two."

He calculated for a while. I could see his lips moving.

"Address?"

I gave him my address and he wrote in his little notebook. Another cop was doing the same for Delsing.

I put out my hand for my wallet. With something funny in his blue kind of hardboiled-egg eyes he pushed my chest, tipping me on my heels. Awkward and angry.

"Okay, you're under arrest, Small."

"Pardon me, what for?"

"Obstructing."

"Obstructing what?"

"Obstructing me. Now shut up and get going."

IT WASN'T EVEN a black maria, only a little panel truck with a steel netting between the cab and the back. Delsing and I sat in the back. I was trying to keep track of where we were going as the truck turned corners fast. It was a short ride. The home of the police was not far off from Mickey Chang's café.

We were let out and I saw we were in the back of a big building, and then we were held by the arms and taken in a door that led straight to a white elevator. Visions of movie hospital emergency rides. Inside the elevator there was an old man who handled the controls (ex-cop or ex-con?) and he didn't look at us at all, no curiosity. The elevator made the whine you always hear in movie jails, high and lonesome.

We came into a long narrow room where there were many cops in blue shirts. They took us up to the counter where a tough young cop sat tapping a pencil on a pad of paper. He had a brown crew-cut and a white scar running across the top of his head.

They finally let go of me and let me stand there by myself. I didn't feel good. My head was starting that kind of around the edges and between the eyes business that comes when you've been drinking and you didn't get high. Two cops were still holding onto Delsing somewhere behind me.

"Name?" said the crew-cut cop.

I told him.

"Age?"

I told him.

"Height? Weight? Colour of eyes? Colour of hair? Any scars or identifying marks?"

I told him, I told him, I told him, I told him.

"Occupation?" he said.

"Student."

"What?"

"I go to the university. "

He looked at me as if he was going to slap three aces down on my three kings.

"It ain't doing you much good, is it? You can't even learn to keep out of trouble." And he wrote with his pencil.

Theoretically I had always hated cops, at least for the past ten years or so, and I was learning to dislike them the better I got to know them. When we were kids Delsing and I said we were going to be policemen, guardians of the law. We thought they were the men they were made out to be in comic books and radio shows and movies—good guys who rounded up crooks because they wanted to make the world and its society safe from danger and destruction. But that was before we met any. In the years we were at college we had met a lot of cops and we had seen some of the things they do. Once in a while we would see them ganging a kid, usually a Negro or Indian kid, and the cops were not protecting anyone, not even in their abstract minds. They were enjoying breaking bones and making blood, because they were killers and gangsters who could wear uniforms and guns and they could shoot a man and claim it was in self-defence or because the man was trying to break away. We had heard that a lot of men had been killed in this police station, and that they were usually trying to escape, or they had died of natural causes. We knew it was a lie. But there was nothing you could do about it. Even if the public heard about it and politics entered and there was a cleaning out of the most depraved and sadistic cops, there would be a return to the same situation, because in most cases it is a certain kind of personality that takes a job as a cop. The ones in the squad cars were usually more intelligent and human than the ones walking up and down the sidewalks.

Now it was more than a theoretical hate I was to have for cops, and this is not the blind hate of a junkie or a bum. Remember I am a college student. I am concerned with the crap our society shovels down its own throat.

"National origin?" says the cop behind the counter.

"Canadian," I said, remembering like a flicker in the back of my head that this was a sticky business with the government up top.

"College student, eh?" he said, his mouth like a great sucking chewing thing of flesh. "What's your national origin, college student?"

"My father was a Canadian," I said.

"The only Canadians are the goddam Indians," said the cop behind the counter, as if he had manufactured the idea on the spot.

"Then the logic makes me an Indian, I guess," I said, dragging the last words down my collar, a little afraid now, not knowing why.

To ease out of my uneasiness, I leaned forward to see if he was writing down Indian, and thinking *Jesus they're really going to put me in there this isn't just a scare routine thing you get on the street and then don't let me find you again yes sir officer I'll go straight home you son of a bitch cop.*

His fist was up over the counter, pencil squeezed in it, in my face.

"Get your head away or I'll clip you one."

Steel all around me, I noticed, great walls and corridors probably flecked along with cells and bars and groaning men in them grabbing bars and looking out or rolled in a corner, and I was going to be in there. Well, maybe it wouldn't be too bad, I would get right to sleep because I needed it, and be pushed out on the street in the morning. Bright sunlight. Tomorrow didn't look too bad.

"...put them on the counter." I picked the voice up. How did my attention wander at a time like that? As probably I was dramatizing, seeing me from the out-context, looking like a layout for a scenario or something, like Delsing said his second self always stands away looking at him when he's making love or wiping himself on the can, his most intimate moments, he calls them.

"Sorry, what did you say?" I was trying to be polite and offensive in it, so as not to sell myself out. I must have been a little drunk at that.

"Take everything out of your pockets and put them on the counter. Belt and tie too."

"I'm not wearing a tie."

"Come on, come on."

The voice was getting dangerous, I thought.

The place was awful bright, I noticed that all of a sudden, as I fished the stuff out: sticky old handkerchief, dirty gummed-up comb, they already had my wallet, change that was only eighteen cents, all I had, pen, notebook (thinking *God don't let me lose that there's valuable stuff in that I gotta get it back they'll probably look at it and think I'm some sort of queer*) and cigarettes. I was going to wish I had a cigarette later. A cop took my glasses off me and put them on the counter. They had beer stains on them.

Another cop started to pat and feel around me: I stuck my arms straight up at the sides like a shakedown derelict hobo hood in a TV show. *I'm just a routine like everybody else case for them*, I thought.

"Put your hands down," the cop said, ominous.

In a normal voice I said, "Aren't you trying to humiliate me?" Arms down.

"I'll humiliate you all right," he said, a threat. I wondered what he thought the word meant.

He took the belt from Delsing's old air-force raincoat I was wearing, jamming his big hand in the side pocket and taking out my gloves and one big button that had been in there for a couple of years. I said I was sorry I had forgotten them.

They must have finished because the big guy had a hold of my arm and was starting to take me away. I saw Delsing at last, standing quietly in the doorway with his cop, standing there like a spectator at a play that would break into some kind of violent disaster kind of catharsis if you only waited quietly enough. But I saw him in a blurry Goya kind of way, and it was partly because of the stuff I'd had to drink, though that was a long time ago, and I was sobered by the business at hand, and my eyes were hurting me a little, promise of a headache in the morning, if there was going to be a morning.

I pulled away from the hand in my armpit a little, and I leaned back to the shaven head at the counter.

"Can I have my glasses?" I said. "If I don't have my glasses I get these headaches." Delsing wasn't wearing his glasses there in the doorway, I all at once noticed. "If I go too long without them it has bad effects, I get these headaches that hang around for days."

"No you can't have them, shut up," said the tight mouth in the flaccid face.

'Would you explain the rule against glasses?" I asked, scaring myself a little. Time was stretching thin, showing little tearings in the elastic pulling of it. I knew.

They were grabbing me now, one big dark-uniformed policeman at each arm, pulling my arms hard around to my back. The third one came around from somewhere, very neatly, speedily, deftly, driving three or four hard short fist blows into my abdomen, and I was sagging down on the arms of the cops behind me; then there was no time, I caught a sideways glimpse of Delsing standing aslant in the doorway as they were hauling me as fast as anyone was ever hauled, one cop at each ankle, me bouncing along on my head and shoulders along the white tile floor; then they flung open a door and slammed me up against a wall, dropping my feet on the floor, throwing them down hard. My head felt cracked open jagged in the back, and in a moment it was oozy. I watched like a baby as they grabbed my shoes off and stuffed me through the door. The door slammed with a faraway echo and a huge white light came on over me. Steel footsteps marched away and I could hear my breathing.

I was in a kind of white tile closet and I was cold, the way you get lying on tile. I lay on the floor, unable to stretch out. It must have been four feet by five. I measured as well as I could, thinking *details get them exact for the exposure remember everything they think you're too drunk to be able to tell anyone in the morning will I get out in the morning*, and I looked upward, measuring. It stretched up, very high. The light went out.

CHAPTER TWO

THERE WAS NO light in the cellar, it was another of the things in the house that didn't work, house of women and sad secrets, so she carried a lantern down into the damp place, concrete walls holding back the ooze of ocean maybe, or maybe total collapse. It was just hacked into the ground and somewhat fortified, a hole made big enough for shelves of fruit jars, some of them years old, old cardboard cartons of college books, a couple baseball bats, old boxes full of rubber boots and army jackets that no one would ever wear again, things that would inhabit the earth for all the years it took for them to crumble into unrecognizable parts of the mash after time. A long time after she too would be dead. Her face hit a spider web, and she lifted the lantern, old camping-trip tent light, hissing in the damp hole. At face level the dark tunnels stretched out past the light down between damp beams of dark wood, the floor of the living room it was. The dog whined upstairs and the sound came from an odd angle and stopped.

It was in the box under the apricots, cardboard box split down one corner. She pulled it out and sat on an apple box beside it, the apple box itself a thing brought from the other place ten years ago. Old magazines, college papers, clippings yellow and brown with crooked typesetting, cobwebby envelopes addressed to many of her relatives, all came out of the box, and she piled them beside her. The album was right at the bottom, loose-hinged, flecked with gold design that used to be a maple leaf and CANADA embossed, cheap thing, thick, bulging in the middle with pages crooked, showing corners flapped and torn, dull brown paper, soft. Most of the pictures were brown, with fancy old-fashioned twirly edges, or the corners rounded off. All documented with white ink, with dates and scratchy writing, pictures of old prairie combines and frame houses and black collie dogs, Saskatchewan and Alberta scenes, people standing in polka-dot dresses and thick trousers, stiff 1920 postures, dead photographs. She turned the pages slowly, moving the lantern closer, closely looking at each figure, trying to find something, construct something.

There wasn't a camera in the house now. No one wanted to take pictures of it all. She lit a cigarette and the sharp sweet smell hit the cold air of the place. It was the best-tasting cigarette in a long time. The men were posing in love with the women, arms around them from behind or elbows linked standing side by side, smiles and serious young people looks, splendid attempts at glamour, a record for always of these people important to themselves and all coming events.

For ten or twelve pages there were no pictures of anyone but the two of them, standing together, all taken with the same camera, all printed by the same old studio. In bathing suits, in driving clothes, in funny tennis outfits, in the car, in the hills, by the beach, on the front porch, in front of the merry-go-round at the circus, the two of them smiling at the camera and at each other, recorded lovers posing for the slow camera, for the brown pictures. He was tall and slim, curly haired and athletic, with clothes a little flashy, picture-taking clothes. She was short and a little plump, beautiful in long ringlets, dark-haired and frilly bloused, looking out quietly and leaning to his chest, a nineteen-year-old girl herself then in euphoria, stunned by love.

She closed the album and stuffed all the things back in the box. The cigarette burned her fingers and she dropped it on the damp floor. The water in the pipes was running. The dog was skittering around on the kitchen linoleum. At the foot of the rotten ladder she stopped and lowered the lantern. It was a lizard, staring painfully into the hissing lantern with bead-red eyes it couldn't close.

CHAPTER THREE

THE LIGHT CAME on hard and I cold see eyes looking at me through a three-inch glass hole in the door. I had not been asleep, but I had no idea how long I'd been in the closet. Somehow the cold that had gone all through me from the tiles was part of the same thing that wouldn't let me have any idea what time it was. I looked stupidly at my wrist where the watch had been removed hours ago, or whatever. There was a hard ache in a layer through my head, and my belly sent a sick feeling up to my throat, the athlete must have developed a good underbelt punch at police school. The door opened and there were two of them there, the guy that grabbed me in the café, and another. My cop was waving a long blue paper which I thought I was supposed to look at, so I reached out my hand, and the cop yanked it back. I expected Athlete to come around the corner swinging his fists. My cop took a self-righteous smile off his face and opened his mouth a quarter of an inch to talk to me, the hardened criminal leaning against the wall with one hand on my gut, staring down at my dirty shoes against the wall outside.

"You can make a statement but you are not compelled to everything you say can be used against you," the cop either said or asked.

I looked at his piggy face for a second, then back at my shoes.

"Do you understand the charge of obstruction," my cop either said or asked.

"No, I don't," I said, looking at my shoes. The laces were still tied. Imagine that.

"You're going to stand trial under that charge, buddy."

"Were you one of the guys that beat me up?" I asked, giving unneeded emphasis to the gasping I was doing.

"I ain't seen you since I brought you to the station, buddy." He folded the mysterious blue paper.

"Can I go to the bathroom?" I said, hunched over and holding my stomach like a concentration camp regular.

"I guess you better," said the other cop, sounding like a pretty ward nurse, comparatively. They told me to pick up my shoes, and herded me to another door across the hall. Through the door I could see three bare toilet bowls without seats. I said thank you and entered the room. The door slammed metallically behind me and a heavy lock banged into place. I was in the gloomy can, freezing to death with my shoes in my hand. A derby hat and I would have been a slapstick tragedian.

After finishing awkwardly with the toilet I put on my shoes and looked for a place to wash, but of course there was none. The water in the john had splashed against my ass so cold I had fantasies about ice forming. I knew I was going to spend the night in this lavatory, so I looked through the dull light for a nice piece of tile to stretch out on. It was a long room, and most of the place was taken up with steel double-tiered bunks. There were about twenty men in the room, some hunched in corners on the floor asleep, some sitting together smoking. They were all one colour, brown, befitting my experience of the room, and they were all the same featureless shape, blobs of men in the ninth circle of the city's underworld. I walked down the room, looking for a place to flop, knowing already that there was going to be no sleep for me in that temperature, not against tile and steel anyway. It must have been about forty degrees. I began to wish I was lushed to the ears, I always sleep well when I'm full of booze, under any condition, with anyone. There was one top bunk left at the end of the room. I climbed up, lay down, and tried to pull the thin raincoat around me. The claustrophobia started moving in, and it was the first time I ever felt it. It was as if the walls were some Kafka machine, ready to push together and gunch us all together like insects.

I was lying on a straight slab of steel with holes the size of fifty-cent pieces cut in it, no covering, no head rest. I remember saying to myself in the old Small-Delsing fashion: *Well, here I am in jail.*

And as time laboured on it got colder and colder. Some men were huddled together on the floor, trying to gather each other's stinky heat. Everyone looked like the derelict father of someone. I saw a cigarette glow somewhere at the other end of the room, and I was acutely aware of a cigarette hunger. I put my hands behind my head and looked up at the ceiling, where I could see large messages burned with matches, profane insults for cops and boastful signatures from drunks long time ago. A cop came in and shone a flashlight in everyone's face, making sure everyone was awake and alive. They wanted to have everyone looking as bad as possible for the trials in the morning. That was why they took away the combs. I could hear the prisoners talking over their arrests and probable convictions.

"I was standing in front of the liquor store with fifty cents, and I come up to this guy and asked him if he wanted to put in fifty and split a bottle of wine, and he flashes his badge and I'm in for panhandling."

"Happened to me once. I ask this guy if he can lend me five cents to make up bus fare home, and he grabs me for vag."

"Nice guys."

"What you in for?"

"Bugger off, will you?"

"Leave him alone, eh?"

"My fifth vag. I'll get six months in Oakie."

One man was lying on the floor near my bunk, propped up against the wall, fussing with his foot. He had his shoe off, and blood was seeping out all around his dirty old work sock. When the cop with the flashlight came around again, he shone the light on the red smear and walked right by. When he put the light in my face, I was staring with no expression right at his eyes. He was about twenty years old.

Lots of things. One man ran to the door periodically and pounded on the steel with his fists, a little man, screaming for his diabetic pills, begging, hollering he couldn't make it to morning if they didn't give him back his pills. Once he asked the cruising flashlight cop if he could have one of his pills, and the cop shoved him up against a steel bunk and hit him between the legs with his flashlight. Another little guy ran around all night hollering that he was sick, proudly pointing out to the talkers where he had puked against the wall in a corner. You could complain all you wanted, this you couldn't help knowing, and you wouldn't get looked at till the next morning, not if you had appendicitis. *Natural causes.* For instance, the guy in the bunk under me made loud bubbly groans all night, each one of them coming up at me through the holes in my slab of steel. The junkies, two of them, sat quiet against one wall, knowing the uselessness of asking for help, knowing it from other times, the action going on inside them, all the action of their lives, pumped into them from a needle, decided with the push of a thumb.

Hours later it must have been morning, because one guy came around with a mop and a slop pail, wiping up cigarette butts and congealed puke, and the other guy came with breakfast, which was grabbed quick by most of the cons, the talky ones anyway. The guy with the bloody foot just looked up once, too tired to move. Breakfast was two pieces of toast done about an hour before, and coffee heavy with cream in a metal cup you couldn't hold even after the coffee was tepid. I ate one piece of toast and left the other on my bunk. All night long a smell of urine had lingered around me, coming from the steel slab. Now the smell of coffee mixed with it. Before I could drink the coffee, trying to hold on to it by wrapping the tail of the raincoat around it, a guy came and called my name and told me to follow him. Out into a hall where a clock said six in the morning, into a room where a homosexual fingerprinted me, holding my hand with his fat fingers and pushing my fingers hard into the inkpad. He patted my ass as I left his brightly lit room. It was obvious he liked working with cops and prisoners. Back on my bunk I waited for the rest of the crap that was coming. It was all getting deeper all the time. My thoughts were running to Kafka, and I finally got the nerve to ask for a cigarette, which I got right away, a nice long full tailor-made, thinking *Okay I am one of you, compadres, and Whitman*. Pretty soon a guy in a uniform came in where I was smoking away and started talking to me, holding a writing board in front of him and checking off all sorts of things. He was a white-haired guy who talked a lot quieter than the normal cop. He took all my particulars—What's your name, what's your charge, how many convictions. How was I going to plead, he wanted to know.

"I can't afford to contest the charge," I said sweetly, trying to get a little sympathy. I'd never been in jail before.

"What about the obstructing? Was there anything other than verbal?" he wanted to know, checking things off madly.

"No."

"Well, I'd advise you to plead guilty," he said like a father. "You'll get a light fine at most, it's nothing serious that I can see. And if you've got no funds, you'd better request time to pay. It'll be okay."

"Thank you," I said, in a kind of bewilderment, and already wishing I'd had time to drink the tepid coffee before they took it away.

He turned to go. "Oh, your friend Delsing is pleading not guilty," he said.

Nice guy, I thought. Who the hell was he, I wanted to know. "Salvation Army, they got a good thing going with the Law," said one of the talky cons.

A fat cop with an army moustache came in, hollering that anyone that wanted to could phone for bail. I said I would, and followed him out to the phone in the hall where he stood watching me like something out of a summertime TV program. Undaunted, I picked up the receiver.

"Incidentally," I said, my finger stuck in the ABC hole, "how much is my bail going to come to?"

"The usual—fifty dollars," he droned.

I hung up the phone and went back in the tank. We hung around for four hours, listening to one another regurgitating breakfast, until ten o'clock, when we were split into two sections and herded off to the little chambers next to the court rooms. I caught a glimpse of Delsing as he was walking along with a group to the courtroom down the hall. I would have waved, but I needed my hands to hold my pants up, having no belt. I knew this was another of the cop devices to make you look disreputable in the dock. I wished I could comb my hair. It was kind of long, for a part in a Brecht play we were doing way up there at the university. I wondered where Delsing had been all night. Maybe he'd got a cell with a mattress.

As we waited in the chamber, twenty of us, a cop came through and asked us how we were going to plead. When he came to me I told him I was going to go in guilty. It was a cop word, anyway. Most of the cons said "guilty with an excuse." Every once in a while a name would be called and someone would go into the courtroom between two fat moustached cops, and another guy would come out and tell everyone what he'd just got. I waited and waited, through a noon hour when the court closed for lunch, though we got none. I was finally called around two-thirty in the afternoon.

In I went, catching a short whirly look at the surprisingly small room, oak panels on the walls, little gallery like in a Methodist church, big desk up front, with a skinny old man in a striped suit sitting at it crooked. Up came a cop and herded me away from the dock, where I was headed in my half-feigned confusion. He guided me to a place in front of the big desk, and I stood there, shaking a little, everything was going too fast after the long wait. The big cop with the moustache held a writing board in front of his belly and asked me how I would plead, and I said guilty, looking up at the magistrate. Then I had to stand there while the young brush-cut prosecuting attorney read off his statement. Mounting hate crawled through me as the guy told how the cop reported that I was belligerent, had made arrest of my friend nearly impossible. He said I shoved the cop around and swore at him, threatening to smash him around. The young guy didn't look at me once. I looked around for my cop, but he wasn't there.

I think the magistrate knew what was going on, he was looking at me, and I really poured it on for him, mutely suffering agony and impatience. Everything stopped when the old guy broke in and said impatiently that it didn't sound much like I was trying to obstruct anything, and he was a little tired of these cases showing up in court. Strike the plea of guilty from the record, he said, it was a serious charge that could get me two years. I almost wet my pants, and then I felt as if the magistrate was a spy for the people outside. Before I knew it, they were phoning the university to see if I was lying about being a student, and I was out on an adjournment without bail. They told me to come back in a couple weeks. I felt pretty good.

Upstairs I went again, back to the room with the long counter, and I picked up my stuff from a brown envelope. I didn't get my comb or my eighteen cents. What was Crewcut going to do with my comb, I wondered.

I was feeling a little cocky, and I wanted to go through the thing bit by bit, so "What about my comb and eighteen cents?" I asked.

"Sorry, they're not recorded on the form and I can't do anything about it because I wasn't on duty last night," said the gray-haired guy behind the counter. They covered up for eighteen cents, then. I wondered if he got a cut.

I GOT TO the front steps of the place at 3:30 in the afternoon, dying for a cigarette, afraid to bum one or I would be in again on a vagrancy charge. I didn't know that I wanted to spend, throw away, another day of the blasting sunshine that was laid all over the street, Main Street in the cool winter daytime, strange deserted place for old bent Chinese men in running shoes and black serge overcoats, too many cops and lawyers strolling this way and that way between coffee breaks, straggly girls who worked in the dreary cafés around the street drag, whole canyon of bad decaying buildings giving up the smoke and dark ravagings of the noisy night before, bodies lying on mattresses behind second-storey walls above pawnshops and cheap clothing shops, jammed tight with dusty stuff in the windows, guitars, overcoats, suitcases, jack-knives, fishing reels, old green-covered books, behind smeary windows holding off the dark interiors from brassy traffic of the street, stores with wooden floors and gap-toothed neon signs pushed too close to one another over the open doors. I waited and I wondered what Delsing was doing. I wanted to get back uptown, away from Main Street, but away from cops more. I looked up the street and my car was still there, with a blue ticket under the windshield wiper.

The big glass doors behind me opened and I thought Delsing and turned around, but it wasn't, it was a girl. She stopped right beside me and fished a cigarette out of a burlap handbag, then pulled out another and handed it to me, the first time she looked at me. Thanks, I said, and reached for matches but I didn't have any, and she had to dig in that bag again, holding one foot up on the toe, burlap bag on thigh, and hunched over, digging in a slippery pile of I guess cosmetics and stuff, and came up with a box of wooden matches, the kitchen kind, long ones with red tips, and I lit us up.

We stood there side by side, smoking, looking out at the street, squinting in the sunlight, and it was a little funny, but I was tired.

CHAPTER FOUR

THEY GOT OVER their fights fast because they were both afraid and relieved that it was probably just a summertime thing, and they raced each other into the incoming waves. The water was warm at the edge and cold where they plunged under and swam out. They swam hard and evenly, out farther and farther, past the big low-tide rock and out into the high waves. Saltwater filled her mouth and she felt it bitter and clean. He stopped but she swam by him, laughing, and he struck out after her. Finally he caught her and they stopped to look back at the beach. It was a long way back, and she felt the soreness hit her thighs now, her heart beating fast as the waves pushed her up and down. He was grasping and trying to shout something, but a wave crashed into his open mouth, and he ducked under, comically stricken.

She felt him touch her and he came up behind her, spurting water in a sun-shining arc into the air. His hair was plastered to his head, round head of an athlete. She ducked under and swam to him and bit his leg. He churned water and she saw him coming down after her. She had no breath left, and he caught her. He held her and they bobbed together, kissing. A boat motored by, and someone was waving. They waved back. The sun was shining down brightly on the water.

Somewhere the white whale was rising vertical out of the water, skyscraper in the sea, Ahab tied to his back with a crisscrossing of ropes lashing him tight like a baby on its mother's back. Sea spray cascading from the giant flesh.

They floated on their backs, talking to each other, far out from the white sand on the beach. He was wearing his white bathing suit, wetted tight to his body, and she reached out and rested the back of her hand on his chest.

"I'm tired," he said, fluttering his feet to keep them up. She didn't have to move, lying on her back. Her toes and the pink bathing suit loose over her breasts out of the water.

"I'm not tired," she said. "Look at the clouds long enough and you will be in the air looking down at them, you'll be swimming in the air, not the wet water, look at them long enough and the idea you have about walking with your feet on the ground will slip away from you in the waves. Maybe our ancestors flipped out of the sea because they wanted to know which way was up."

"Incidentally, you're crazy."

"I told you that at the start of the summer, and you said that's the way you liked them."

"Stupid thing to say. I can't believe it of myself," he said. "Wish we had cigarettes."

"Why don't you swim back and bring them out?" she said. "And don't forget the matches."

"Why don't we make love out here, instead? Can you float for two people?" He swam to her, holding her hair in his hand, dipping little handfuls of water over her forehead with the other.

"Why don't you just look at the clouds?" she said, then she ducked under the water and swam away from him, coming up and resuming a floating position.

They had just started to make love a few days ago, after a long wait, over the edge and now joining frankly, enjoying each other as much as they could, talking about it all the time, exciting each other in as many ways as they could devise—new love, warm and surprising, experimenting love, days cycled around the pressure of their bodies together, everything seen from the perspective of their wonderful new animal. She had never slept with any man more than one time before. She looked at him now, muscular spermy man, lying on the water.

"I want you," she said, murmuring it straight toward the sky, to him, the whole world, voluntary envelopment in him, as in the sea, the white whale, propelling itself out of the water, great hunky body relentless against the air.

"God damn," he said.

"What?"

"God damn, you sound like Uncle Sam. Sometime you will stand beside my bed pointing your finger at me and glowering and saying in red letters, I Want You."

"Pooh, you can't take anything straight, you have to corrugate it with that mind of yours. You could use a little Ahab in you."

"What the hell is that?" He was a radio announcer. He didn't know half the things she talked about, and he didn't care, and neither did she.

"My way of saying I hate you," she said, scudding her hand in the water and splashing him.

"You know?"

"I don't want to listen."

"I want you too. Let's go."

She got a head start and yelled back at him, "Last one to shore has to use the small towel!" And she swam as fast as she could.

All the caught-up pain in her muscles eased out now in the stroking through the water, she had no time to look at the peaceful summer scene, and this was the way she liked to see everything, in gyrations of her head wet from the splashing element she strove through, mighty whirling dash to the land, sunshine mixed with clean water in the frantic and graceful splashing where they met, and where they met was her body, doing its doing with no time for mental reflection, it was the whirl and the effort of this moment. And he was behind her, splashing with his bigger arms and legs, mightily testing his sheer masculine strength against her, depending on it, and with her too, accepting her joy in the complete effort in which she could win, but then secondly, nobody wins if your effort is total, because total is winning and the muscular driving through the water is the prize of life, the moment, the obliteration of all else.

It was the way she was in love, mightily, totally striving with the gyration of all, eyesight open to all the colour and movement of the absolute moment, the obliteration of all else, making love as she swam now, in competition with him and in the consequent total activity with him, telling him with all her movements and cries and guarded silence that he had joined her in her stance against the world. She impelled herself harder and harder through the water, entirely given up to pressing herself to her all-out speed, enjoying every stretched movement of her muscles, in love, beating beyond the white whale, streaking to the shore, and never looking back, seeing only the whirl of water and sun.

Till she felt the soft sand touch her foot, and she stood up, bashing to the rim of the water, laughing loudly, gasping with the beating of her heart high in her chest, propelling herself to a last forward dive onto the dry towel, lying on her belly and laughing shrill and waiting for his heavy body to hit the towel hard beside her. Till the moment broke and glided away and she turned on her elbow to look back, laughing the recovery light laughter, reaching to push the little towel up into her hair.

There, the whole empty sea and cloud, he was not there, no head in the water. Her laugh hit back and she felt the heart thumping in her. She looked and he was not there, he didn't come up, and she stood, looking at the water. It was too long, he wasn't under, he wasn't playing with her. She ran into the water on her aching legs, swimming hard out again, feeling the pain now, looking hard at the water, seeing shadows in the waves.

CHAPTER FIVE

THE BRIGHT COOL sun looked good on her face. How can I describe her, or do I really have to? I guess you've seen a lot of girls who have maybe one or two of her characteristics, especially if you've ever hung around the places of young culture in Vancouver, and maybe other towns the same size, city places where there is a crowd that sings folk songs, paints big red and black canvases, reads Camus and Dostoevski, and makes it on the local theatre stages or tries to horn into television. Not the teenage crowd that goes bohemian for kicks, the edge of college and art school people, the ones that go to beer parlours instead of house parties. She wasn't university, I would have seen her in the cafeteria if she'd been out there, because she was the kind of girl I always look at hard in a group. I always look hard at girls who are attractive, so to speak, with something a little quirky about it, like prominent cheekbones, or a flat chest. I don't know.

What was there quirky about her? I hesitate—maybe I could lead up to it, round about, me all the time now hoping Delsing would be a little more delayed coming out of that steel and concrete place, he'd be hollering for a cigarette, I never saw a guy who smoked so much, especially on other people's cigarettes. The burlap handbag is a starting place, and I guess her clothes, to give an idea. She had on a pair of flat black shoes with white ankle socks touched with dirt smudges. Upwards, a felt jumper thing, green felt, one of those things with no belt, goes over a white long-sleeved blouse, looks good on a young girl who is nice and tall-looking and thin, necessarily. On her it looked young and honest, you'd have to say, something I want to describe because it is always with me, the way these things look, not a jumper necessarily, the way certain unglamorous clothes can look so fine on a girl if she's the right girl, you'd have to have it yourself, this feeling. Sometimes a girl can look just right with pigtails, beautiful but not pretty with make-up and delicate features, everything made by an expert: beautiful. Like a well-touched-by-human-hands English car rather than a sleek glossy Detroit model. I guess if you haven't figured out what I mean by now, I have lost you.

Her hair was short, almost straight but whisking around in little tendril curls, around the temple to the forehead tendril, short, bits tipped up behind her ears, a few jumping around on the top of her head, it was thick hair, light brown and bright, giving off energy and light reflections of a kind of blonde, and you could tell she didn't have to comb it much, didn't want to, that was why she had it that way. Lovely, not unusual, just enough. Her eyes, where I have to go next, looked down, away from me except that once when she handed me the cigarette. They were there between blue and gray, the kind Delsing would call irrevocably green if he saw them, and when I thought of that I got nervous, then thinking what about that, you've only just seen her for half a cigarette's time, a nice girl sure, but you are in not exactly top condition after a night on a slab of cold steel, out of the morgue into the frying pan—it wouldn't have sounded like a bad idea for a while in the middle of the night. Her hands were good, with short nails, and her body was flat, with maybe a bit of nice firm round curviness at the bottom. Her legs were straight anyway, with the provocative slight swell of the calf that I alone seem to appreciate—it's one of those things, some guys fix on Cadillac bumperettes.

"You waiting, too?" I said finally, thinking what is she thinking about me hanging around here. And me thinking the same about her, and she probably—well.

"I'm standing. I never smoke on the street," she said, not looking at me.

"Just on cop porches, eh?" I said.

"Any objections? Are you a cop?"

"No, I'm on the side of humanity, being a new ex-con," I said, trying like mad to be friendly.

"What's the matter, you trying to be a social protester?" she said, puffing smoke out and catching it in her nostrils. Looks better than it sounds.

"No, I'm trying to make friends," I said, cool.

"Well, I just got out of jail, friend."

"Well, so did I. I obstructed a cop twice as big as myself."

"You're pretty big," she said, turning to face me. It had worked, whatever it was. I was thinking I'd tell Delsing about this, and he would go into the old tirade about how I fell in love with a girl when she asked me directions to the post office.

"I was in for being a prostitute in a public place, for flaunting my young body in a place called the Elite Café, for lewdly offering my sex for public consumption. I was having a cup of coffee in a Negro café and a cop came in. Later on he tried to put the long arm of the Law around me, and got nothing but a thing a nice lady in the next cell called a vag. The fatherly judge gave me a reprimand and the prosecuting attorney gave me a leer. They didn't give me back the dollar and fifty cents I had in my bag when I checked in."

"I paid eighteen cents," I said. "You must have had the executive suite."

"I don't like you," she said.

I took a chance, something I'm not accustomed to.

"Knock off the espresso-bar manner," I said. "Talk like a person."

"Now I like you," she said. Everything was working, I didn't know the secret of my new power. Maybe it was the night in the can. I began to worry about what I might smell like. There wasn't any sink in the can.

Then that damn Delsing came along, pushing the double doors out in front of him like an archduke, as is his wont. He looked out at the panoramic street and said: "So this is what it's like on the outside. God, look at the modern cars!"

"Hi, Dels, old friend," I said.

"Gimme a cigarette," he said. I gave him my butt, about a drag's worth. He puffed it and chucked it into the gutter.

"Let's eat breakfast," he said.

"No money," I said.

"There's a bill under the floor mat of your noble car," he said, leading the way, old resourceful, much-travelled Delsing.

"Wait a minute, wait a minute," I called after the fiend Delsing, who was striding off down the sidewalk with the determination of a man trying to forget something. He turned around and looked at me, dropping his shoulders dramatically.

"Well?"

"George, we have a guest for breakfast." I put my hand on her shoulder, and she walked out from under it. She was looking at Delsing, hostile. "He's really a pretty good guy," I told her. "He just gets like this when he's spent a night in jail."

He came back, and was suddenly foppishly gallant. I hated him at times like this, and he knew it, but couldn't stop himself, or so he said.

"I'm sorry," he said. "Forgive me, I've been under a bit of a strain. My name is George Delsing, the hungry and cigarette-desiring George Delsing."

She opened the bag and gave him a cigarette, giving me one too. "How do you do," she said.

"This is..." I said, in the old movie-time manner, slightly inclining my body to her.

"My name is Andrea," she said, and we all turned into the nearest café.

CHAPTER SIX

"**ANDREA DO YOU** have to sing that same song over and over?" screeched her mother from the front seat.

Her father said nothing, only the back of his head visible as he looked straight ahead, driving the car, he the car driver, enjoying the little problems of right turn up hill, more accelerator, ready to brake for the sharp turn, whole weight and thrust of the machine enclosing them controlled under his fingers, the car in good shape, a little draggy, feeling of raw power. In this way he could shut them out, and this was visible to her in the back seat, seeing this easy stillness of the cleft between the tendons in the back of his neck, under the flat brim of the old-fashioned hat, this neck that must have shown dark against the pillow, against the white shoulder of her mother, just that once or twice.

"I like the song," she said. Fretting in the space of the back seat, playing with the long-dead cigarette butt in the open ashtray, seeing outside the long miles of open space of the inlet and the wooded pine islands out in the fall-away mist. Upper Levels highway for the Sunday Drive, feel of moving up from the city, high enough to see the ocean spreading out like an ocean dropped there and seeking its level. There were little sailboats standing still down on the water, white triangles.

She opened the book, humming the song again.

> *Death, or distance soon consumes them: wind*
> *What most I may eye after, be in at the end*
> *I cannot, and out of sight is out of mind.*

"Property values are going to go up fast out here," said her mother, gloating over the open rocky and tree-touched land beside the road.

"There's a nice view," said her father.

Bobby stood on the floor beside her, his little hands holding on to the seat behind his father's neck. He had remains of some kind of ice-cream sundae on the corners of his mouth. She looked at him, thinking how easy it would be to reach out and clean his face. But you leave things, if you will only leave things and look at them and let them be as they are, the world doing its doing. If the door is open, leave it open.

Eagle Harbour, butte-rounded rock cropping looking over the old Spanish sailing place, two hundred years of water lapping rock piling logs now scrubbed and smooth against the beach. Hopkins seeing morning's minion dapple-dawn-drawn Falcon, the sun opened itself up, the water deep below was a mighty big ocean from Eagle Harbour. There's a nice view.

"Seagull, seagull," said Bobby, two and a half years old, second family kid fifteen years younger than his sister, his father's dark neck against the pillow another time, and X begot Y, he was a beautiful child, too young to know the trouble of being a Harrison.

"Seagull, seagull," she replied, playing with the cigarette butt in the ashtray.

"If we had been smart we would have bought out here ten years ago," said her mother.

"If we'd had the money," said her father, enjoying the pull of the car around the top of a rise.

"I had the money," said her mother.

Andrea sang the song, little, tearing the cigarette butt with her short thumbnail. You don't have to file your fingernails so short, her mother said, heavens above you're a girl, you know. Don't we have enough of not knowing the simplest things in this family? Organization, don't you mean?

"Andrea," said her mother.

"I'm very sorry," she said. "I think it's a nice song, even if it hasn't got much of a moral."

"Do you want to walk home?" said her mother.

Yes, yes, yes, yes. Try me

"Notice how the gray water on the rocks suddenly gets blue. There's a line," said her father. Andrea knew he was saying it for her.

"Bobby! Quit playing with the door handle," said her mother.

The car turned and crested another high rise in the road, and the sun reflected off twenty miles of ocean like a gigantic piece of tin. Underneath were the miles of unexpected dark, deep heavy oceans full of distant fish, unknown to the world, swimming only. No finny tribe here nor fish magic Klee creatures orange in the corners, but flesh heavy under the eternal push of water. Under the bridges of Vancouver deep water went to the full ocean, out, under, into place.

"Why don't you read some of that?" said her father.

"We're supposed to be getting fresh air and sunshine," said her mother.

So she read:

When will you ever, Peace, wild wooddove, shy wings shut,
Your round me roaming end, and under be my boughs?
When, when, Peace, will you, Peace? I'll not play hypocrite
To own my heart: I yield —

"With this new highway, there'll be garages and drive-ins and all—before you know it, poof! up go the property values," said her mother.

"Yes! I do!" she shouted.

"What's that, dear?" said her mother, turning in the seat.

She just stared at her mother, feeling the anger and frustration escaping around the edges of her eyes.

Her mother was wearing her Sunday Outing clothes, tight tweed suit and white gloves, flowery and trim hat stuck with pins on top of her twisted light brown hair. She was wearing heavy make-up and her lipstick pulled tight to the corners of her mouth, her eyebrows were pulled and plucked thin. The earrings gouged through the flesh, cruel instruments of a superior heartless animal. Mrs. Harrison was one of those strange small-town women who have not been changed by fifteen years of city life. She still ordered all the big glossy mail-order catalogues.

Bobby pulled the handle up and the door opened, the road went by underneath, forty miles an hour, and he stepped out, down. Her father's arm came back and his white hand grabbed Bobby's arm, the only thing to reach, and Bobby came up, back into the car. Her father slammed the back door and continued driving, slower now. She hadn't been able to move. She held Bobby against her.

"I'd like to see if you'd sat still if that book of yours fell out the door," said her mother. "It's a good thing somebody had the wits to move when it was needed," turning to look down out her side window at the property values.

"I push 'em in and I pull 'em back in, too," said her father, short of breath.

CHAPTER SEVEN

"**WELL, WHAT DO** you think?" I said, sitting back as Delsing drove my little car slowly along Burrard Street.

"I think I'd like to change my underwear," he said, squirming in the seat for emphasis.

"I mean about Ann?" I said, determined.

"I thought it was Andrea."

"All her intimate friends call her Ann."

"Ah, knock it off, Small," he said.

"Come on, have you ever seriously thought about the real possibility of strong affection at first sight?" I said, losing ground.

Delsing reached up and twisted the rearview mirror around for me. "Have a look at your present first sight," he said.

I looked and twisted the mirror back. "What's a couple whiskers?" I asked.

"I'll admit that at the best of times you attain the giddy heights of mere ugliness," he said. "But this is depravity, obscenity, perversity, a festering insult against the whole race of man, a blow to the cause of human evolution, a menace to the principles of good taste. You look pretty bad."

"Get pretty giddy when they let you out of jail, don't you?" I said. "What did you get?"

"Another date in two weeks, same with you?"

"Yeah."

We crossed the Burrard Street bridge and traveled up Fourth Avenue, leaving it all behind us, moving up and out to the university district. We had classes in the afternoon—no, this was Sunday, we had classes the next day.

"Jesus H. Eisenhower!" I shouted, startling Delsing and almost careening us into the lane of cars coming the other direction.

"What?"

"I didn't get her address or even her last name."

"Small, why don't you think?"

"I dont know, I guess that means I'm in love."

"I mean why don't you think now, you boob."

"What do you mean, Herr Doktor?"

"How many girls you know with the first name Andrea?"

AND HE WAS right, it didn't take me long to find her. I managed to hold off that night, but the next night was Monday night—no, it must have been Sunday, they couldn't have had us in court Sunday morning—and I'd been working on Corneille all day, desperately trying to feel for the old French that came dribbling into my inner ear, angrily yanking down the old green roller blind to shut out the eager early-spring-wintertime sun, emptying mountainous piles of cigarette ashes and apple cores, listening to the radio news every half hour to ease me away from the old green book for a few minutes, listening to the light syllables that flashed around inside my forehead like the light bulb news headlines that travel around the Hotel Vancouver: ANDREA...ANDREA...ANDREA...ANDREA...

So about seven o'clock at night I couldn't go from Delsing's spread of fried spare ribs back to the smoky air around my desk lamp—I got up and dawdled over to the couch, lying down and placing the telephone on my chest.

"Gonna wash the dishes tonight?" said Delsing.

"Think I'll make a few phone calls first, talk to a lot of people I've been neglecting recently," I said.

Delsing brought the last beer from the fridge and poured me half of it into a tumbler, or nearly half, I guess.

I diddled with my finger in a dial hole for a while, then dialed the Nancy Chan number—what the hell, she knew our old thing was a when-you-need-to-talk-to-someone thing anyway. And she knew a lot of the arty farty crowd.

"Hehrro," came Nancy.

"Hehrro, Nance, this is good ole Bobby Small, remember me?"

But she didn't know any Andrea, though she thought it sounded like a nice name. Lovely Nancy, flower of the Orient, catty claw-woman of my dreams. So I called a guy this time. He never heard of the name, in fact or in theory. I began to worry that she had given me the treatment, a moment's dalliance, a cigarette handed out as you would drop the last bite of your sandwich to the mute staring dog under the table. Whoa, I thought, running my nicotine fingers through my hair, scratching my itchy scalp, thinking I don't care if her name is Phyllis Schwabb, I'll love her as Andrea, high in the Andes mountains of Brazil, Portuguese love songs playing in her hair, strange fugitive girl of my Sunday night. Then I hit on the genius procedure; I called the swingingest folk song club in town, exulting over my new-found flashing wit as the line buzzed the first three times. It kept buzzing. Sunday night, everything closed, fate plunging the ice axe into my skull.

I lit a cigarette and burned my fingertips with the match, and called ten more numbers. No Andrea in town. I called ten more and gave up. Then I called Maureen.

Maureen was the heart pulled through the mouth, love I threw away in a time of great self-love, good friend we both said now, thing that was a lie when we were foolish enough to see each other in the same room, at opposite walls, trembling with old knowledge. It was a specially bad time just after the imagined end. When you are alone with a girl you used to sleep with, there is a giant excitement, you suddenly both know nothing but that body under the clothes, and you know you will either leave and feel like a Victorian novel, or you will have the old soft lifting of the sheet and momentary unbearable excitement, white lights exploding in the back of your head. A few times we had done it, the best ones we had ever had. And a few times we had tried to come back to each other, at first experiencing the blast of love hotter than ever, when you walk down the street looking in the crowd for her face, stabbing your glance into every face, every figure, looking for your girl, a chance meeting downtown, though you know that you would recognize her out of the crowd four blocks away. But it had always fumbled down to the same old place, jealousy and self-love, the blast finished and more interesting things to do. I had loved Maureen more than anything, and for a long time Maureen had been the third part of this apartment, the cook bringing her huge platters of spaghetti to Delsing and Small, the boys feigning great starvation, heaping abundant and extravagant praises on the girl cook. Maureen had been an institution and a love.

"Hello."

"Hi," I said.

"Oh, hello, Bobby." Her voice bringing half-pitch the old intimacy and warmth.

"Just thought I'd call and ask how everything's going. How's things at the art school?"

"Fine. What did you really call for, Bobby?"

"Well, darling—"

"Maureen."

"I'm sorry, force of habit. Maureen, I just wondered if you could help me locate someone I'm looking for." This was going to be a peculiar situation.

"What's her name?" asked Maureen. I had always been dismayed and awed by her intuition and her unfaltering frankness.

"It's just that there's something I want to tell her, you know."

"Come on, Bobby," she said. "You never used to slough things off, that's one thing I always liked you for."

"Maureen, there is so much—"

"I didn't ask you for an explanation, did I? I just asked you what her name was," said Maureen, good Maureen, better than I'd ever known, or maybe better than she had ever known while we were still together. She was more beautiful and more concerned now that it was over.

"Okay, her name is Andrea." I tried to get the slight pride and wheedling out of my voice.

"Is that all? Andrea who?"

"That's why I called, I don't know any more. She's a kind of not quite overwhelmingly lovely, but with the edge of something odd, you know. And she seems like a young anarchist organization girl, you know what I mean."

"You must mean Andrea," said Maureen, and I knew I was going to get what I wanted.

"Yeah, that's the one," I said. "Andrea who? And where?" And she told me. She knew Andrea from a few years ago. And I knew why the subject had never come up between us.

"Goodbye, Maureen, I love you," I said.

"You always did, remember?" she said, and she had won again.

But I got a little back by hanging up before I could say something really stupid.

IT WAS IN one of the condemned streets of the West End, among the funny old houses that were dying shells, unimproved because the huge glass apartment blocks were coming closer, most of the places up rickety old staircases, where you would find no heating except old woodstoves in the kitchen, places where on weekends a hundred bottle-clutching actors and painters and poets would congregate in dark standing clumps and listen to guitars and social protest songs and Miles Davis records. The people that lived in the places were usually painter husbands and schoolteacher wives, unemployed ex-students getting a cheque for twenty-three dollars from the government office every Tuesday morning, young married couples or common-law couples working for as little money as they could, trying to have beautiful children and cooking the best-tasting meals in town, especially great German green salads. There would be second-hand-store furniture and homemade drapes, and huge old kettles on the stove for the hot water, usually a big room with half-finished canvases and a mattress with a blanket. This was the place where students in the art school wanted people to think they lived, but where actually the real producers of seldom-sold art grouped together, moving when their building would get the orders of demolition, to another up the block. Funny old-fashioned buildings, where stairways started in the strangest places, where the rooms were all crookedly leading off each other, the windows round or hexagonal, the light switches peculiarly out of date.

I found the building, a great brown wooden thing reaching up narrowly three and a half storeys, with a turret at the top front, and I knew then that the turret, circled with eight little windows, would be her room. To get in the place you would have to go around behind a little art gallery and along a broken wooden walk, to an outside wooden fire-escape, and up to the second floor. Washing hung on a railing that stretched along a boardwalk to the roof of the art gallery building, where there were more rooms. Lights were on all over the house. House of love.

I thought I'd been there before, probably on a party after a party on a Saturday night in the fall. But they all looked alike in their odd singularities, it could have been any house on the block.

The reason I am hesitating to tell is the reason I was hesitating then, the feeling that I was doing something I wasn't used to, as if there was a kind of hypnosis or guiding power, and I was watching myself from away. Usually I got into relationships with girls, but it was by falling into them as they were convenient or inevitable, as they would just happen. I had never been a guy who went out and mapped a strategy in the good old fashion of the American movie or magazine. I had once known a guy who said he just went up to girls and asked them if they wanted to fuck, and I had asked him if he didn't get into a lot of trouble that way, and he said yeah but he also got into a surprising number of beds. And here I was hesitating, wavering between the me inside the good old comfortable tank of myself, and the me being watched by myself from the outside, a little surprised. Till I saw her figure in the window of the turret.

I walked up to the first landing of the fire escape, and turned the funny little bell clanker on the door there. I turned it three more times, each time getting a feeble grinding clank that couldn't have carried much more than across whatever room was inside the door. After a long time a man about thirty years old, wearing a tee-shirt and paint-splattered jeans, opened the door and squinted out at me standing in the sombre light. A wave of hot air came out the door.

"Hello," he said colourlessly.

"I came to see Andrea," I said, trying to sound like a guy she had known for a long time.

I wondered who this guy was, naturally, and I tried to look at him edgewise, not wanting to appear scrutinous and therefore outsiderish.

"She know you're coming? I think she's in bed."

All the time I was hoping like mad this guy wasn't her husband—I'd never thought of her having a man or a husband. I hoped he wasn't anything else, too.

"You're not anything else, are you?" I asked, then seeing that he looked puzzled, "I mean, I haven't known Andrea very long, and I kind of hope she isn't yours."

And this was unlike me, too. I talk funny a lot, and like a stupid bungler very often, but not in situations like this, not in this kind of situation where I was feeling so inexperienced.

"No, she just lives here, friend of my wife," the man said, without humour. He was probably a good painter, I thought.

"Well, maybe I could come back," I said. Thinking of Andrea's figure in the window above, and all the time a little nervous, thinking how comfortable it would be driving the little Morris Minor across the bridge, back into the homey part of the city.

"Come in, I'll see if she's up or something."

The guy went around a corner and up some stairs. He came back down and stuck his head around the corner.

"What's your name?" Direct as always, I thought. Probably paints big canvases.

"Bob Small, but you better say The Convict. It's sort of our nickname for me."

"Bob Small." And he went around and up again.

All alone, I lit a cigarette, wondering why I didn't hear any wife around, the house was so quiet. I could see into the next room where there were two unmade beds. There were more than three people living there, I knew.

He came back and motioned for me to climb the stairs. I came around and looked up, seeing the stairs bending to the right, out in a circle out of view.

"Just keep going till you come to a door," he said, and I started climbing.

The door was slightly open, old rusted story-book door, and the light I'd seen from the street was on inside, and she was there.

"Come on in, Bob Small!" she bellowed from inside across the room.

It was a funny little turret room, filled mostly by her bed, a high thing with no posts, sumptuous mattresses topped by a slinky blue taffeta cover, and four or five pillows. There was a bookcase made of apple boxes nailed together, and on top a small mirror propped against the wall. Books were all over, lying on the floor, propping up one of the windows, stacked along the bottom of the walls under the windows. With all the windows it was like being in the middle of a beetle's eye, you saw out in all directions, a funny feeling of height and surveillance over the city, viewing down on the spill of False Creek into English Bay. It would be that way in the daylight. At night it was a surrounding dark.

She was sitting back on her heels on top of the bed, with her knees fanned out, roly-poly thing in a pair of yellow cotton pyjamas, the legs of them rolled up above her knees, she looked younger this way, but sweeter too, so that I wondered if she really had spent the night in jail down the hallway from me. And she wasn't as flat-chested as I had thought when I saw her in the jumper, so I thought she probably hadn't been wearing a bra that time, and I knew right away that was probably just like her; because now when she moved I could see a swing of breasts against the loose cotton material.

"Here, I owe you a cigarette," I said, handing her the package.

"Is that why you came?" she asked, looking at me directly, resting back on her bent legs, comfortable.

"I owe you a light too," I said, flicking my lighter and moving it under the tip of her cigarette, dangling from the middle of her closed lips.

"You're a college student, aren't you?" she said, and I knew she was aware of everything. "So why aren't you studying?" She lolled onto her stomach, leaning on her elbows, face toward me. I could see down the front of her pyjamas, and she lifted one foot in the air, leg bent at the knee, nice curving calf of the leg...

"I've been reading French all day. But I kept wanting to get out of the house, take a look around the West End."

"And you decided to drop into my bedroom for a chat. Do you like Schoenberg?"

"I don't know," I said, remembering from flighty campus cafeteria talk that Schoenberg was a modern composer, and remembering how I didn't like the way the talkers worked to pronounce it. *Shernbairg.*

She reached down on the other side of the bed and flicked a lever on a tape recorder. The music came out, twirling cello and violin all alone music, drifting like a girl's hair on the water.

"I like it," I said.

"Sit down, then," she said, and I sat on the end of the bed, taking off my jacket and dropping it on the floor. I looked out the south window and I could see car lights moving across the bridge, and farther away the yellow blob of the city hall clock.

"How long have you lived here?" I asked.

"Ever since Leonard and Audrey said I could. About four months now, I guess. Ever since my nineteenth birthday."

"Haven't you got any family?"

"Sure. Hasn't everybody?" She laughed like a hurt person, dry and short, broken at the end in flaky syllables.

"Well, how come you're all by yourself and going to bed so early on a Sunday night?"

"I'll tell you what," she said. "I think that's none of your business."

She rolled and rocked on her hips front down on the heaped up bed, a pyjama-ful of curvy girl. I was getting an erection, and I hoped I didn't have to stand up too soon. Think of something else, Bob. All I could think of was roll rounded thighs and curvy hips and the touch of hard fingers.

"I'm sorry," I said.

"Don't be so goddam stupid," she said.

"Okay," I said.

"Okay."

"You sure got a lot of nice yummy books here. If Delsing saw them he'd fall in love with you. He always says—I like to have books ALL over the place! One time he was yelling that and flinging out his arms, and he smashed a lamp off his desk. So he used mine for a week. It's because he's older than me and he's the leader of our two-member club."

"I don't think I like him very much."

"Aw, he's always nervous when he's around girls, thinks he should impress them, and he always bungles it. Actually he wants everyone in the world to like him."

"Maybe he shouldn't be so damn conceited. You're not conceited. Just enough, that you don't even know about."

"What are you?" I said. "A psychiatrist?"

"No, I've just seen a lot of them operating."

"You getting analysis?"

"Up till four months ago I was."

"What happened four months ago?"

"My mother and I had a disagreement, she called the cops, and I left the sanctity of my home. It was my nineteenth birthday. She had a nice idea for a birthday party, don't you think?"

"You don't get along with your family, eh?"

"I don't get along with my alleged mother, that's all. Nobody does, especially not my alleged father. He and I don't know each other, my mother wouldn't introduce us. I just knew there was a strange man around the house."

"My mother died when I was a kid, and my old man ran away from home, the lucky guy," I said, trying to partake of her world in my own small-town way.

"Aren't we a sad generation? Bombed out by the ravages of war and the resultant discarding of morality and tradition."

"Now you're talking the way you don't like people talking," I said.

"I don't like myself, that's easy. You *do*."

"I like you, too," I said. "So you've got a responsibility."

"Aren't you going kind of fast? You know when I first talked with you, I could have sworn you were shy and not so quick with the ladies and otherwise," she said, scuttling forward on her belly and taking my cigarettes out of my shirt pocket. I lit hers and took one myself.

"Honest, I'm just as surprised as you are," I said, trying to sound surprised. I was surprised, but part of what surprised me was my suave manner. If Delsing had been there he would have been taking notes like mad.

She leaned back against the wall at the head of the bed, smoking like a girl. Her bare feet, clean and pink, were right by my hand. I touched her little toe, and she wiggled her toes, wiggling me away.

"How do you like my room?" she said.

I'd like to move in, I wanted to say.

"I wish I had one like it," I compromised.

Illusions, illusions, we have them all the time, people like me. I was day-dreaming in her very own presence, this girl, day dreaming that she would say move in, get over on one side of the bed, gently undo my pyjamas, turn off the tape recorder, touch strange skin to skin, set up eternal housekeeping here, and forget the world.

"You'll have to go now," she said.

"Aw!" I was incongruous or maybe impolite, depending on this girl I had known for a long time that was a day.

"I have to work in the morning," she said simply.

"What do you do?"

"Well, not what they had me downtown for doing when I first met you. Not quite."

"Thank god for that."

"Yes, I suppose. Actually I only prostitute my mind. I do my time at a neighbourhood house."

"What in hell is that?" I said, not liking the sound of it, but pleasantly aware of the minor verbal irony.

"A place where snotty-nosed kids learn to play the violin after school."

"Well, that's lovely. I mean I'm glad, that's a neat thing for you to do," I said, serious as I could get.

"Yes, isn't it?" she said, picking at a toenail, breasts pushed against her upraised knee.

"Well, I guess I better be moving off," I said.

"I've said that," she said in her straight manner.

"But I'm going to see you."

"Okay."

I wondered if my new-found brashness would jolt me into trying to get a kiss on those pushy lips, but my mind saw the clumsiness of failing, getting dangled by the shoulder straps as she pulled away, fantasy of my nether mind, old ego-smashing plague of my private dreams. I succumbed easily and smiled my way out. Down the curving staircase like a visiting monk out of the queen's prison. Andrea you are a queen. What are you doing, looking for a fat lip? Down and around the corner is the man with the painty jeans, Leonard Samaritan the good-hearted

Levantine with a wife who was away. I smiled at him, and he looked up at me from where he was sitting, dark intellectual horn-rimmed glasses down a bit on his nose, dark eyes looking up at me over glasses and under lifted sharp-angled eyebrows, hair receding a little on top of tanned head. Skinny denim legs crossed, feet in maroon wool socks. He held his skinny homemade cigarette in the middle of his mouth and looked back without a smile.

"Guy's gotta be nice to her," I said, hoping like mad I was saying the right thing.

"Yeah," said Leonard, thinking of me as a bad figure on a big painting. "Nice to her."

I yanked out a cigarette and headed for the door. Leonard didn't see me out. I got out and into my little car before I looked back at the turret. The light was out. She was in bed or looking out the window. I ran the motor longer than usual.

CHAPTER EIGHT

SHE PULLED THE screws out and put the full-length mirror on the floor. The room seemed to tip without a lurch and the ceiling came into the mirror a little crooked. The edges of her eyes caught more yellow wall than before. Swimming season was over and white bodies lay waving back and forth in the long green weeds, long hair trailing wet with tendrils among little fish and fugitive underwater green sunshine. Winter was ready with its cloud-bank out on the Pacific rainwaters and the cold air of fall was settling in over the city.

Poised over the mirror, she looked down ten feet to her face looking down to her from ten feet above. The figure in the glass was wavering, ready to fall, to sail, to come out and away, swaying on the edge of adhesion, out of the world in a second, it was herself seen from within the glass and out to the yellow walls.

The telephone rang in the hall and she deliberately waited while the bell came ten times then stopped. Telephones don't often ring ten times, it must have been something important to someone. But there she was in the mirror on the floor, now with nothing on but pink panties and pink bra, solid legs apart, hands on curves of hips, hair undone, short and scatter-curled, alive hair, after a summer of saltwater swimming. The calendar on the yellow wall had a page of April and a painting by Miro, red child's writing against white sheet, blue boats and red scrawl of writing with name Miro in thick-rope-coil child's handwriting in bottom right corner reading up the page. April in the springtime with the unturned pages of summer underneath—Leger, Matisse, Bracque, Tamayo, Rivera—unturned, uninterred, unsunk in the salt.

She stood at the window and watched the cars moving along the street, dusky September light and car lights picking at each other along the white line, the driveway empty, parents away in the evening dusk driving to Granville Street, store windows full of mirrors, sunset destroyed by massive bank of purple clouds, imagery of fall night, sky full of airplane lights, everyone beating the arriving dark.

She turned and walked across the cool room and turned on her tape recorder. Sonny Rollins saxophone things filled the room, licking out farther each time, moving against the corners of the yellow walls. There was the intelligent masculine blues and her bare legs. She bent and lowered one arm and stepped out of the panties. Then her shoulder bones jutted out in back like nubile wings as she reached her hands back and snapped off her bra. Her breasts dropped heavily out of the gentle lace cups. Sonny Rollins licked his way through a solo, saxophone rising in melodic jabs into the air, saxophone sounds.

She stood over the mirror and looked down at the reflection. Somebody could have been standing at the rail of a bridge. Rain could be falling on bodies in the park. It could be summer in the world, somewhere. The quartet was in the middle of the blues.

The glass was cold against her skin. She flattened herself more, pushing away the cold, and the fronts of her shoulders pressed against the glass. She lowered her open mouth to the open mouth.

CHAPTER NINE

ALL THE WAY home from school on the bus Monday I had to stand up in the thick aisle crowd, pushed up hard and swaying against a tall girl in a wool suit. At first I was thinking only how glad I was that Delsing had asked me for the car to drive off to some kind of archaeology digging, down toward the States. I held myself just slightly against the stops and starts of the bus, knowing the third or fourth time that the girl was knowing this too, and there was an interim of understanding between us, strangers taking something unpremeditated and soon to be gone forever, a surprisingly human moment of secret and luxurious joy at the tag-end of the day, the two of us looking away in opposite directions, angles and soft places of our bodies meeting in short and ready moments of passive tolerance and enjoyment. I looked at her once and she looked at me once, and we both knew it was a funny world in the city.

Making me think of Andrea, of course. She was a girl you could tell had been busy moving all over the city for years unknown to me, her small body next to big buildings every day while I was doing something else, Andrea maybe stopping for a sandwich in the basement of the Hudson's Bay store, sitting down in a chair I had left a moment before, me now looking at books on the floor upstairs. Our bodies meeting briefly, casually in time and space, moving in the fluctuations and flows of downtown crowds and moving afternoons.

Tonight, I told myself, I have been planning to read the other two acts of Molière, periwig dusty side-of-the-mouth humour, all manners and two hundred years away, filled in the brown cupboards of time, in another country, dear to another people, disinterred every year at this time for a few hundred more college students way at the west coast of a continent too damn young. And I knew I was trying to convince myself. Here it was the beginning of the week, five days from the weekend, too close to the end of the spring term. Delsing always saying for Christ sake, Small, there is no weekend in my life, no end of a term cut off by a sharp exam paper, don't measure little pieces of your life, just start gobbling and keep consuming till you come to the end, there's no ration books you have to keep balanced. But I didn't work that way, though I wished often that I did, and knew I never would. For me, everything has to be accounted for to the shadowy parents of my mind. I've always had a father fixation on my own conscience, this a sort of perverted kind of self-discipline, an excuse.

And so of course I also had a guilt complex about reading Corneille and Racine and Voltaire, and I had a guilt complex about not reading them, too. Delsing was always saying for Christ sake Small the reason you get those French guys to read is because they are accepted by the phony French crowd that teaches them in English-speaking universities, because they're all eunuchs, they don't endanger the mastery of the blackboard brush, they picayune around all the time about manners, which is a Gaul god. They don't say a goddam thing. For Christ sake read Villon and Rabelais and Bloy. And Delsing couldn't even read French. But my conscience father was saying yeah he's had his showoff say, now get down to reading the other two acts. It was better to think about girl problems.

Which was Andrea, I knew now, because here it was three days anyway I had known about her, and the lights were still spelling out the news round and round in my head every peaceful moment.

"You know I'm going to be glad I went to jail," I told Delsing.

"You're a nut," he said matter-of-factly, without raising his eyes off the girlie magazine he was reading or looking at.

"I'm glad I got beat up and everything," I said, dreamily.

"You're queer for prison guards and cops."

"Else I wouldn't have met Andrea."

"Else you wouldn't have met any prison guards, either," he said, turning the middle page sideways and looking at it calmly.

Which meant in our parlance that he was kind of glad I was getting my mind off my studies. If he had said anything about her, it would have meant there was something wrong. He should have gone into business.

So I didn't get off the bus till it was downtown, and now the choice was up to me. I could go up to her place in the turret, and I started thinking a girl like that, what's the symbolism of a turret, or I could go to second-hand bookstores and later pick up last month's *Figaro*, and later have a hamburger and beer in a pub, and later console myself weaving on the seat home on the bus with the fact that it's always good to take advantage of situations and get your second-hand book buying done while you're in the neighbourhood.

Falling in with my late unaccustomed brashness, I decided on the turret. I started walking over to the West End, saying to my father, I'm going to get at old Molière first thing in the morning, I'll get up early. Liar! came the resounding answer.

She was sitting on the fire-escape of the old-green-stain house over the little art gallery, and so help me god she waved and smiled as soon as she recognized me coming around the side of the building in my baggy pants and misshapen hound's-tooth jacket. I waved back and trotted athletically up the steps to her.

"Hi, Andrea," I said.

"Hi, Bob Small," she said.

"You can call me darling," I said, borrowing an old Delsing line, which she must have realized, because she frowned.

"There you go already," she said.

"Sorry. Doing anything?"

"You know, for a college man, you ask some pretty stupid questions," she said, but it was friendly, she was smiling as if she really wanted to be nice with me. It was a big step from our last meeting. Maybe because there was more room out there than in the bedroom.

"Okay, here's one. Why do you live in a turret?" I said, leaving out the rest.

"Wouldn't you want to live in a turret?" she said reaching in my shirt pocket for my cigarettes.

I can think of one I have my eye on was the instantaneous thing in my head.

"You know, for a neighbourhood-house girl, you answer some pretty good answers," I said, gallantly.

She stood up.

"I was just waiting for someone to take me walking down to the beach," she said.

"Here we go," I said, giving her my hand and helping her up. It was the first time we had ever touched. Her hand felt wonderful, that's all. Everyone knows that feeling, but it always comes as a surprise at the touch. I let her hand go. I was thinking of the wool suit on the bus.

Walking we went, the long way, seven blocks to the beach where the long lawns ended and there would be an end of parked cars full of people. The sun was low out on the water, and long lines of shiny ripples came in toward us, the light you like to see girls sihouetted and running along the beach in. But it was cool, there were no girls, just Andrea, and the light was slanting on her, so I had to get her between the sun and me, I wanted to see the light picking through blonde in her brown hair, a gilt edge all round the soft hair on her head, picking light edges at it where it sprang up lightly in those little curly ends, hard to describe, but everyone has seen them.

"You know—"

"Shh-shhshh..." she said, shaking her head a little. Girl getting her will and this didn't happen too often, I could tell, or didn't used to. Four months: somehow I had a knowledge she had a lot of catching up to do. So I didn't have to make talk. In recompense I reached out and took her hand, and I got that wonderful touch again. It was a deal, and we walked down to the edge of the water with our hands tight together.

We stayed quiet a long time as the light descended from red to green to the dark blue of coming night, and the gulls weren't shrieking anymore. Till she finally said something.

"There's a lot of water."

"And that's just the top, there's lots more underneath, too," I said eagerly.

As if she hadn't heard me, she was thinking along somewhere, out on the water somewhere it seemed.

"You really dig the ocean, eh?" I said.

She pulled her hand out of mine, gently, but in one motion. She walked a few steps and sat on one of the big smooth rocks that crop up out of the sand. Her legs were stretched out toward the water, tight black slim-jims catching in wrinkles at the tops of her thighs. Muscular legs and long thighs that curved outward a little in front, the way I like them.

"You know something? I'm going to tell you—I like you, Bob Small."

"I was really hoping..." I didn't want to go on with that. "I'd like you to know I'm glad about that," I said.

Thinking to myself, I don't know what I did right, I wish I could I don't know keep track of what I did right for future reference but who cares about future reference...

"Last year I wrote a hundred poems about the ocean, and I scratched them all out," she said suddenly.

"Delsing writes poems," I said.

"Does he scratch them out?"

"Not very often," I said, wondering why it sounded like an

apology or at least a reluctant admission. "I think he's a pretty good poet."

"Of course, you love him," she said, simply.

"Yeah, but—"

"I didn't say you slept with him."

"We been friends for twelve years," I said.

"You're lucky," she said. "There's not many people have been friends that long."

"Cigarette?"

We lit up, tasting the good taste of a cigarette at evening beside the beach, old-time taste, like the good outdoor taste of cigarettes when you're just learning to smoke.

"Andrea, I've got an idea that I should say I haven't got, but if I said I didn't have it I would know I still had it, and I don't get very many ideas like this, so it would be a shame to waste this one, and saying I haven't got it won't put it off anyway," I said, stretching it out I guess because I didn't want to stop and actually get to the point of anything, afraid I suppose, the old me showing through the new me.

"Bobby," she said, holding her hand out to me again. I took it and got the touch.

"Gave myself away, huh?" I said sheepishly to cover my nerves.

"Bobby," and it suddenly struck me that she had dropped the Bob Small bit a way back. "The last two boys who asked me are dead now," and she looked out at the sea, her hand unconsciously turning back and forth in mine.

But she was such a little girl, she was a nubile brown-haired tight-packed lively lovely bunch of jumping human being. A little girl. A sweet little girl, untouched by the rough brush of real life, too little and too young to have met half the people on her block. What the hell was she talking about, especially to me, small-town boy from ole Lawrence where a stabbing murder twelve years ago was still being buzzed about and the hotel it happened in avoided by local residents?

Say something for god sake say something good, I was hearing in my head, my mouth meanwhile working like the mouth of a guppy inside a glass case, nothing coming out.

"I didn't want to get involved right now," I said, about the stupidest thing I could think to say, and the first.

"I don't want to get involved either!"

So I had to, I put my arm around her and all of a sudden her face came down to my chest, and my other arm went around her, holding tight. She wasn't shaking, so I couldn't tell if she was crying, but I suspected that she was, crying quiet tears against my chest, the awful kind of very still crying. I held her a long time and it got darker around us, quieter.

Her hands were against my chest, beside her face. I put my mouth down beside her ear, feeling or sensing a whole softness from her.

"Let me be the one who goes places with you and talks to you, and happens to be there all the time," I whispered.

I was surprised and happy to feel she was nodding her head there against my chest.

"And we'll leave the getting involved till later and see, huh?"

She nodded again.

CHAPTER TEN

THE BIG BUILDINGS were different from the way they were in the pictures in the newspapers back home. There was more than just the seeing of them, there was a way they were real, real stony hulks and between them traffic that moved by, safe and full of people that didn't pay any attention. Along the sidewalks pigeons walked in thick groups in front of her, and she looked at them fixedly, seeing the movement of their muscles sleeked over with feathers, as real as chickens. Nobody walking along the sidewalks seemed to notice the pigeons, they walked right on by, the way a farm boy walks past a barnyard of chickens, but here they were real pigeons and tame enough to be a part of the city, part of the strange sea-smelling city where sounds were sharper and continuous, where the cool fresh feel of the sea was strange and exotic to a little girl from the hills. Mostly it was that the people here were so calm and quick about knowing how to do things without figuring them out or even pausing to notice how complicated they all were—people knowing how to push the paddle to open the doors on the streetcars and buses, knowing how to wait on curbs and go when the yellow light from the side goes off and the green light in front goes on, knowing how to do all the shopping, all the café eating, all the bus-catching without having to think. People's unconscious hands holding silver bars in the streetcar, woggling bodies to the stopping and starting of the buses, men holding newspapers folded down the middle to read the news on the way home on the streetcars, people walking past the legless beggars on Granville Street without noticing them, red-coated old white-haired man stopping a taxi in front of the hotel doors. She wondered how the taxi drivers knew when to stop for people on the sidewalk, because she never noticed them signalling. She was bemused and she kept it a secret from her mother, because her mother had been in Vancouver when she was a young girl, and she was used to all these things, and she would laugh and call her a hick or say don't be silly. Her father wouldn't say anything. He was from a middle-size town back East, and he had seen lots of cities. But once on their first day in Vancouver he had gone chasing a pigeon, and her mother had called to him, and he had stopped.

Because she had been born and raised up to six years old in the little town that seemed to be the only place in the world where of course she was meant to live, other places and big cities being things for newspapers and geography books. She had finally got through one year of school after waiting for years to move into that strange place where older kids went for hours every day, coming down the hill at 2:30 in the afternoon, filled up inside with secret knowledges. And the secret knowledges had become the mystique of her everyday life, and she was glad there were eleven more years of this before she had to leave to a short adulthood and the final death. But now she was going to live in the city, this wasn't just a visit as to the Okanagan Valley that time to Uncle Frank's orchard. There would probably be a school here, but it wouldn't have the secrets she had waited so long for.

So of course she hadn't wanted to come. They had to come because her father was getting a new job, and it seemed to Andrea that there was a power in her mother that was responsible for moving the heavy load of the family all the way over the mountains to the Coast. And there was a thing not explained to her, something that screwed up the corners of her mother's mouth and hung like a thick sheet between her mother and her father.

And part of it was that her father was so quiet all the time they were moving, just working for her mother, man who saw about moving the furniture and selling the stuff they couldn't take. He had an awful way of working quietly, and his eyes always slid away when she went to talk with him. Once when she first knew they were going to move she went to talk with him and ask him why, but her mother took her by the arm and told her to help in packing the dishes.

So they were in Vancouver to stay, all right, and it was because of her mother taking care of everything, and something shameful in the background.

As they walked along they came to the street by the railroad station by the wharves, and the pigeons were thicker in the air. Two little boys on the sidewalk bumped into a tough-looking man in a brown leather jacket.

"Watch where you're going, you son of a bitch!" yelled one of the little boys, and they turned around and ran up the sidewalk.

She had never seen anything like it before. She was afraid for the boys, but the man in the leather jacket just looked up the sidewalk after them, then turned into a door that said MEN on it in white paint.

In front of the railroad station there was a great big metal statue of an angel carrying a dead soldier up to heaven. There was white pigeon stuff all over the angel and the soldier. Leaning against the bottom of the statue was an old man with no legs. He was sitting down, and the stumps of pant legs stuck out in front of him with hard leather patches on the ends. He was dirty and his clothes were torn and crooked.

She had never seen a man with no legs before. She tried to think of her father with no legs, but when she could picture him with no legs, the picture father would start growing legs, and pretty soon he would be walking around like everybody else.

The three of them kept on walking. They came to the pier and watched the big white boat slowly moving away from the dock. It didn't seem to be moving for a while, but pretty soon it was out in the middle of the harbour, and in a while it was under the big bridge.

Looking at the boat going under the bridge, she began wondering if God knew she was moving to Vancouver. God might think it was peculiar her being in Vancouver instead of at home, but then He would have to know this was her new home now, *their* new home. God would have to know about her mother and father moving too, and arrange everything to get used to the idea. It was odd to think of God looking down at her here in Vancouver. He would be the same, though, like a huge man who was friendly just before punishing you, someone you were closer to when you were alone than you were to your parents, and when you were with your parents it was with the secret that God was closer to you than they were, and you would go right back to Him when you were alone for a while.

She wondered if her father had been close to God when he was away somewhere in the town before they came to Vancouver. It had been odd to be in the house with no father, when her father was somewhere in the town. For half a year the other kids at school had had one secret she couldn't get at, and for some reason she just knew it had to do with her father.

"Where's Daddy all this time?" she had asked her mother.

"How about helping Mommy with the garden," her mother had said.

And when he did come home he was like the servant.

The pigeons were hopping around in a tight bunch, all trying to get at a slice of bread that was on the sidewalk up from the pier. One time last week they were in Stanley Park, and she had seen a big shaggy pigeon with one leg hopping around the popcorn stand, and she had looked at him for a long time, letting the ice cream melt and run down on her hand. The man in the popcorn stand said it was all right because old One Leg got more food than any other pigeon in the park.

They met a great big policeman in a blue uniform with a thin red line down his leg, like a mailman. Back home the policemen were Mounties and they had thick yellow lines down their legs.

In school they showed you posters and told you how the policeman was your friend, and how they helped little kids that were lost, and how they protected people from danger. In the posters the policemen were always handsome and smiling and holding a little kid by the hand. But the policeman in the blue uniform had his hat brim pulled down over his eyes, and he looked mean, as if he was looking for a kid to spank or throw in jail for lying or stealing milk money from his mother. She didn't like the policeman, she thought he looked mean and angry.

They got onto the bus, and she made sure she got the seat by the window, so she could watch all the stores on the way up to home. It was a whole half an hour before they would be home. She was glad they didn't have a car any more the way they had back home. The bus was better.

CHAPTER ELEVEN

HE SAID SHE had come in about an hour ago and she was still in there as far as he knew, so I paid my second-last dollar and walked into the fuzzy-lighted gloom. There were low rafters just inside the door and I had to duck my head, so this must have been an authentic place. On the little stage there was a circle of floodlight and two guitar-plunking folk singers were shaking their heads and belting out an Irish song about whisky in a fruit jar. Folk music I can take or leave, and I decided to let the sounds bounce in a cushion off my head while I got oriented, standing there in a little blob of pitch blackness to the left of the second door. The folk singers came to a head-shaking finish and the applause was bigger than it would seem to be from such a small crowd, probably thirty people sitting in the dark.

The lights didn't go up, the folk singers grabbed a banjo and twelve-string guitar and went into an updated Negro spiritual. So I walked around the back of the room, past people standing up against the wall and drinking coffee from thick green mugs. Fish netting hung from the ceiling in a doorway that led out back around the other side of the kitchen hole in the wall. I went out and ablutted in the little closet that had MEN painted on the door just above a similar sign that said WOMEN. Only one person at a time could get in. There were poems on the wall, in free verse.

I found her sitting at a table all by herself way over in a corner on one side of the little stage. Covered by the sound coming from the banjo, I eased toward her. She was sitting at her table, staring hard at the singers, her light raincoat still on. She was smoking a cigarette, and the ashtray in front of her, an old sardine can, was full of butts. I pulled out the other wooden folding chair and sat down, not saying anything. She knew I was there, but she didn't say anything.

So I lit up a cigarette, looked around at the bad paintings on the walls, and waited for the singing to stop, knowing that then she would start talking to me. There were a few small questions I wanted to ask. It was the first time I ever got a little mad at her, and it wasn't very good, because there I was loving her worse than ever when I was mad at her. She looked beautiful in the dull reflection from the stage, more beautiful than she looked in real light, so to speak. She was sitting with her elbows on the table, her fists under her chin, her neck stretched out long in the dim light, and her hair down fluffy over her forehead. I was beginning to wonder if she knew I was there after all.

Finally the folk singers quit singing and shaking their heads, and the lights came up a very little bit as they grabbed their guitars and waggled off the stage fast. Jazz came on, records from the speakers high in corners, some quartet I didn't know. People started talking and the waiters were moving around the tables, carrying trays of milk and coffee and funny things to eat. I waited for Andrea to turn around and say something entirely calm and normal. But she didn't turn around, just lit a cigarette and stared at the stage as if there was still a folk singer there with a guitar and skin-tight suit.

So I gave in. It is my nature.

"You happen to recall anything you were supposed to do tonight?" I asked.

She didn't do anything, as if I wasn't there, or as if I was and I wasn't supposed to be.

"Andrea, it's me, Bob Small, here I am sitting here at your table."

Nothing.

"Trying desperately to make contact with you."

And then she turned around and looked at me, quiet and unperturbed it seemed to me, me thinking *Christ she's flying on juice or something I've got a junkie and I didn't know I had to do that—well here goes another morbid adventure in the sad chronicle of Bob Small of little town North America giver-away of his only soul in the quest to bring a modicum of justice and happiness to the world of the down-trodden and beautiful.*

Till she hunched her coat up on her shoulders and gave me her hand and gestured smoothly that we were leaving, and the crazy notion of the dollar I had just spent came through my mind until I thought yes how right that I should throw away my second-last dollar between me and the end of the month so far away for my girl. Because that was how I was thinking of her though I knew I had better not mention it to her as yet. And out we went, a few faces turning to see who she was leaving with, Andrea, habitué of this place long before I was a shadowy fixture at her side.

We walked along the street downtown, the opposite direction from my car because I wanted to walk with her, wanted to feel how you unwind things that tighten up and pressure you, unwind them walking until there is just the sound of your feet and the unalterable fact that there the two of you are all alone and together in the middle of the city, but better at its edge. We walked a long way, the blocks covered quickly and in silence. She set the pace as I set the direction, walking fast in no direction of her own: And all I could do was keep up. There was something wrong.

Till we came to the railroad pier, a place I liked, so I stopped us and we leaned against the rail, looking down at the water backslapping against the pilings, little pieces of boards and driftwood and orange crates nestled and bumping gently against the pilings. She was beside me with no protest, looking down, not at me. And that was why I wanted very much to get through to her, get the trouble and the silence over.

"Are you ready, honey?" I said quietly, turning slowly to look down at her face, trying to look ready to understand.

"Bob, there's a lot I want to tell you, but there's so much that I—" she opened her handbag, but I had a cigarette ready and lit for her first, "—don't know where to start, and I don't think there's time in the world to do it anyway."

I mused for the proper little time, as if I was thinking seriously, though I was just confused.

"Well, start anywhere, I'm ready to see if there's time."

"Okay." She got a determined look on. "I don't think we should see each other because I'll bugger you up and you'll bugger me up, but mostly the first. I don't care much about me. I knew I had a date with you tonight. Yes. That's what you should expect of me, and now you know, eh?"

But she wasn't looking at me really, so at least she was putting on the hardness. I lit my own cigarette and flipped the match over the rail. Thinking of the cigarettes we always lit, every moment.

"You haven't started telling," I said.

"Okay. Most important to you, I'm a lousy person. All my life I have been, and I come from a lousy family, and I'm sick, and I make other people sick, and I'll make you sick to your bowels. I don't try to be nice to people because I can't be bothered and I don't know how. Nobody ever showed me. My father is a son of a bitch, and my mother is an old whore. Ever heard anyone talk about their parents like that? I wish she was dead, and she wishes I had never been born. I can't welcome you into my family because I haven't got one. The only person in the family that's any good is my little brother, and my mother's trying to turn him into a queer because she thinks that's her vocation. And that man that lives at her house, he's a eunuch. She keeps him beside the dog in the kitchen. The dog's been castrated, too."

And she stopped to flip her cigarette over the rail but it stuck to her finger and dropped against the front of her coat and down by her feet. I stepped on it for her.

"Could you be a little more particular?" I said.

"No, hell, I'm enjoying this too much!" she shouted at me, then looked at me defiantly.

"Shit!" I said.

She started digging in her purse again, and this time she wouldn't take the cigarette I offered her, but finally found her own, and got it lit after four tries.

"Do you like what I'm telling you? Maybe you could tell your friend and he'd write a poem about it. Well? Do you like it?" she said.

"Andrea, I love you," I said, hoping it didn't sound like a social-worker gimmick. I shivered in the cold air from the ocean.

"Shut up!"

"Andrea, I'm not pulling anything, I had to tell you pretty soon, I can't keep it a bloody secret all my life."

"Shut up! Shut up!"

So I decided it was time to walk again, and this time I put my arm around her waist, first forcefully because she tried to shake me away, then as we walked, letting it go gentle. And we walked back up the little hill at the foot of Granville Street, back toward the car.

I was afraid, more than I had ever been afraid of a person. I had never felt this kind of fear, made by another person baring herself like that, baring and hiding. It was not getting better. Not yet, I told myself. I even tried to keep my breathing quiet as we walked up the slope.

We got to the car and I started driving along the streets, the easiest streets, not wanting to take her home yet. There was something sitting between us in the car and I was waiting for it to go away. I remember once seeing a liner leaving the dock and a paper streamer held between a woman on the ship and a man on the dock platform, the streamer pulling tighter as the ship moved out, at last the man and woman leaning out toward each other. And the snap of the streamer.

"All right," I said, "I won't say it yet, I'll hold off till later some time. But would you please start telling me? You know I've told you truthfully how I feel as if every moment of your life up till when I found you, they're all stolen from me, gypped from me. I imagine you as you were ten years old little girl in a short skirt with a ribbon in your hair, skipping with your hands behind you, all those things. I wish I could see them."

"Well, that's the whole trouble, because you want a me that will fit into your *imagination*, and I just have to tell you I don't. Period."

"Andrea, I don't care what you've done—"

"I haven't *done* anything!" She started tapping her knuckles against the window beside her.

I plunged.

"Then why are you scared to tell me about you and the past?"

"Oh, you don't know a goddam thing. Scared. It's not anything to do with scared. It's things you don't understand because you were raised in the sticks in an idyllic and stupid environment, and you think everything is the way you want it to be. I just got it pushed inside, that's all, and I don't want to bring it out any more than it is already. The whole thing is rotten, that's all, and there's no use pushing around in it."

"I've heard people talk like that in novels, that's all," I said, and then suddenly thought that it was all real and people do talk like that and have things like that happen to them, and I *was* living in a world like she had said.

"I'm sorry, Andrea," I said softly, and drove along.

"Sorry for what?" she asked, angry and a little nasty.

We didn't say anything for a while. Then she started talking to me a little more relaxed, resigned, explaining.

"Now you see, that's how I am. I'm not tolerant, and I can't be very nice to people, not even the people I like. Not even to a person I could think I loved. And I like you very much, Bob. But I'd be a bitch to you just the same. Now do you see a little?"

"A little," I said, also calm. "But I'm very sorry, I can't let that keep me away from you."

"What do you want to do? Take *care* of me? Watch *out* for

me? Nice. Be *nice* to me? Because I need *help* so much? I don't *want* that, I'd hate you if you started to take *care* of me and watch *out* for me, and it...all my life there have been people wanting to take *care* of me, and it always makes me hate them. I'm a bitch, that's all. And you won't be any different, don't think you will. I'll be a bitch to you."

"Of course I want to take care of you, but I don't pity you," I said, pragmatically lying a little. "I love you is all, and that's natural. I'm not going to change the way I am, either."

We were at her place. I turned off the ignition and the lights. Lighting cigarettes, I let her cool for a few minutes. Then I made some weak remark about how I hated bucket seats and put my arm around her shoulders as best I could. I leaned over and kissed the back of her neck, as if I were placating her, calming her. She knew this, and she hesitated for a moment. Then she turned her face and I kissed her mouth. Her lips were warmer than usual. I stopped myself from touching her again.

"You know, probably new things are best if you have to have some trouble getting them," I said. I pitched my cigarette out the door and watched the red tip on the asphalt darkness.

She surprised me with a little laugh.

"You know, I love you when you try to be oblique. You're so delightfully clumsy."

"Delsing says my clumsiness is my greatest and only virtue," I said, glad to be talking together again.

"You and he are really good friends. At first I thought there was something phony about it, but I guess you really do see things like that once in a while."

"Sure," I said. "There are nice people and nice things in the world, if you're lucky enough to find them. And if you can learn to trust them."

"There you go. Old obtuse," she said, worrying her cigarette butt in the little ashtray.

"No, goddam it, I wish I could smash everybody that's ever been mean to you in your whole life. It's not a good thing that a girl as nice as you should be bashed around by anyone. I guess that's what you were just talking about, but that's not pity, Andrea, that's because I feel as if someone's hurting my girl while I'm just standing around watching."

"I'd better go in now," she said.

I got out and ran around the front of the car to her door, but she had it open. I was never able to help her with things like that. She always opened her door first or picked things up off the floor. Sometimes it was awkward as I tried to beat her to it.

She gave me her hand now, and we walked slowly around to the bottom of the stairs. There was a light on in her turret.

She started to go up the steps but I took her arm and pulled her lightly to me, old gesture from swashbuckling teenage date days. Her body came heavy against mine and I kissed her hard, making kisses all over her face and neck. I said I loved her but she didn't say anything. It was the first time I had kissed her standing up. The length of her body against me surprised me. She was not the flat semi-sexed girl she had looked when I'd first seen her outside the jail, but a woman with all the gathering power of beauty and warmth of a loving curving body. I put my arms around her tightly, my body seeking all the responding places, and I let myself go, my hot middle against her. She made little noises in her throat, hurt and thirsty sounds, strange to me I thought after the enduring silence of lost Maureen.

We walked up the curling staircase in the dark, her hand guiding me. One step creaked resoundingly and I giggled a little. She turned the light out when we came into her room, and I took a long time closing the door. Then I turned and held her a while, making it easier for us, me. She took my hand again and led me.

"I'll be pretty fast, darling," I said. *Shut up, stupid!*

"That's all right."

While we made love I held her hand. It was the first thing, holding her hand.

"Do you want a cigarette?" I asked, reaching over beside me.

"Please."

We lit cigarettes, and I pulled deep on mine to see her face in the red glow of it. Her face shone with perspiration and the sheets were up over her breasts. I put my hand on her, idle and possessive.

"Do you mind if I say I love you now?" I asked, nonchalantly pulling the covers down to her ribcase. She was shining still. She laughed and it sounded happy. "Well, you'd better or I'll call Leonard," she said.

"Well, I do, really, Andrea."

We took deep drags on our cigarettes and blew smoke into each other's mouths. I would wait for her to say she loved me.

"How was I?" she asked, rubbing her hand on my chest.

"You were wonderful, honey," I said. Stupid word. I kissed her breast and she pulled me to her again.

Later I said, "Can I stay here tonight?"

"I'll set the alarm for six in the morning and you can leave then. Okay?"

"Andrea, I just had a pretty good idea."

"I'll say," she piped up, snuggling to me. I'd never seen her so joyful as she was in her bed with me. I wanted to stay there for days.

"No, I mean about you telling me all that stuff, because I want to know what troubles you. Sounds like I'm trying to unearth your wicked past, eh? But you said there were things, and you seemed to need to get them out."

"I did, when I was going to the doctor."

"I'm not your doctor, which you'll be pleased to hear. It's me I want to help, not yourself, if you want to know. Do you want to hear my idea?"

"I'll listen," she said, lying back beside me, but putting her leg across mine.

"Why don't you take that tape recorder of yours, and unloose into it and leave it for me, and I'll come up when you're at work and listen to it. That way you could have all the time you want and pretend you're just talking to yourself, anyway. Also you could string it together for a novel if you want to go commercial on me. That's my idea. I really mean it, l want to know the things that hurt you and bother you, because l feel as if there's a part between us that's not you and not me alone, but the two of us, joined."

"I'll say!" She sniggered, sweetly.

"Come on now, we said we'd wait a half an hour. What do you think, though, really?"

"No dice, Bobby. Please just drop it, the whole subject. It's not all that bad, and there's nothing you can do about it anyway, so let's forget about it, eh? Please?"

"Okay," l said, hiding my disappointment. "How's about a kiss?"

I was very happy.

CHAPTER TWELVE

SHE SAT AT a table in the city library, leafing through a book on Etruscan art. It was an old brown thing with an old-fashioned embossed cover. There were no colour plates and the brown and white pictures were old-style nineteen-twentyish still-life things with fancy designs around the edges. On the paste sheet in the front the last date for borrowing was in 1941, nearly twenty years ago. She sat turning the pages one at a time, occasionally looking up to see the old men in the smoking room reading newspapers and *National Geographic*.

In the crease between page 72 and page 73 she found a big clipping from a thumbnail, old and yellow as the pages of the book. A piece of another human being pressed for two decades and filed away in the stacks of the city library, moved from the old Carnegie Library to the new one in the West End, transported as with care.

She picked it up and looked through it at the light from the window. Human membrane. A link across twenty years, idle paring of a reader in Etruscan art, masculine thumbnail unheeded and dropped before the turning of the page that would be the last for nearly twenty years. She was the other reader, the second half of the link. If the person had been her age when he had read the book he would be middle-aged now, or nearly. He would be nearly old enough to be her father.

She put it back between page 72 and page 73, and she turned the rest of the pages to the end of the book.

CHAPTER THIRTEEN

WE SAT AND tipped full cool bottles of beer to our mouths.

"How long has it been now, George old buddy?" I asked.

"Two hours and thirty-one minutes," he said.

Since we had signed our names on our last exams and walked lightly out of the armories into the warm noon-hour sun and headed for my gallant little car. Delsing had opened the first bottle while I drove and now here we were in our little apartment listening to Shorty Rogers on Delsing's plastic record player and drinking the cool beer of home. End of the school year, end of exams, start of the summer. Jimmy Giuffre was giuffing his saxohorn and all the furniture stood on wooden legs, all was right with the world.

"Awright, beer, you've had your fun," said old Delsing, and grabbed it with his fist and jammed the neck of the bottle into his mouth. I watched it go foamy foamy glug like the red gasoline in the old pump-up gas pumps of the wartime.

We were kind of looped already.

"Help, I feel kind of naked without my beer," I said. Delsing opened and passed it to me.

"*Con muchas gracias*," I said.

"*Con muchas mierdas*," he replied.

We drank and drank, and sang songs, and Delsing farted

bravely. I couldn't. Delsing said it was a flaw in my character and I had sick innards.

"Here's to Frances and her miscarriage," said George, opening into new territory.

"Let's keep it clean," I said. "Like for instance, what are our plans?"

"Why son, we are going to drink this other box of beer cooling in the refrigerator," he said sagely, gesturing wetly on the floor to the open-doored refrigerator stocked with beer bottles.

"I mean cosmica–" burp— "–lly. What are we going to do when we wake up day after tomorrow?"

"We got jobs, haven't we?"

"We don't know when they're going to call us, do we?" I rejoined.

"Then leave us hope they do not call us before we wake up day after the day after tomorrow," he said wisely.

I was forced to concede the point. Delsing was forced to change the record that had been clucking in the middle for five minutes. On came his favourite record, the Woody Woodpecker Song, ha-ha-ha-HA-ha.

We were going to work for the university buildings and grounds department, hauling stuff and digging places and carrying rakes on the boulevards. It was going to be a grubby summer of work, but we would be in the city, near people that breathed instead of back in dusty old Lawrence, the source of it all. And I thought how fortunate because there was little Andrea Harrison living right smack in the middle of the city, just between the white circle and the first ring in the H-bomb photos down at civil defence headquarters.

It took me this long to realize that either Frances and her miscarriage—which was the reason for her marriage before she had lost the child—were really bothering George, or he was worried enough to dramatize his old position, bereavement, fate-butchered shell of a lover. So I was moved to alter the subject.

"Speaking of Andrea," I said, "I believe I will toddle down and give the girl some smooching tonight. She must sorely miss me, what with all this infernal final exam business depriving her of me for so many days."

"What about this Andrea," said Delsing. "I mean of course this is the real and final thing as they all are, but I'd like to know what's wrong with the girl. Why does she tolerate you six nights a week?"

I put on the face people like to slug.

"My dear fellow, she's obviously taken aback that she can actually fall for a guy is all. She's never met a fellow quite like me before, and she is enjoying her new-found awareness of the woman in her."

"Which means that she's a tigress in bed. Is that what you're trying to tell me, young fellow?"

I belched fastidiously toward him and retaliated.

"Screw yourself, Delsing."

"Damn, I suffer another humiliating defeat at the hands of a wit quicker than mine," said Delsing, wringing his hands pathetically.

I was touched, and tried to alleviate his sorrow.

"She *is* nice in the sack, if you really want to know. I mean if you want to know second-hand, so to speak. But that's not what I meant, at all. Andrea is a terribly good girl who has been terribly poorly done by all her life. I want to make up for that if I can, all I can," I said.

"You deserve a beer," he said, handing me one. And I knew he understood, seriously.

"Thanks a lot, comrade," I said ambiguously.

And so the afternoon proceeded, as we finished the beer in the refrigerator and sank lower and lower in our chairs, until we were lying on the floor, swigging away and marvelling at our own capacities. Outside, husbands were coming home and meeting their families and sitting for supper, postmen were getting on buses for their long rides home, young couples were starting off for the five-mile ride downtown into the city nights.

Suddenly I lifted my hand and fixed Delsing with a blurry stare.

"We must go out and get something to eat," I said.

"And drink," he supplied happily in a kind of oblivion.

"Come on, let's pick up ole Andrea and have a night on the town, buy something special to eat like sukiyaki or frankfurters, come on, come on."

So in a frenzy of activity we got out of the house in another twenty minutes and climbed awkwardly into my little car. Can you drive says Delsing, yeah I can drive when I can't walk says Small and the usual routine is over, and the car bucks and bounces out onto Tenth Avenue and down to the town. It is only then that I discover Delsing has stashed another six beers in the car for just such an emergency, and we keep fluid all the way to the West End.

I stalled the car in front of her place, but we were fairly close to the curb, so I just jumped out and said wait here to Dels and walked as straight as I could around the side of the building. Up the steps awkwardly with a good hold on the hand rail, and I was in the place, not a knocker any more, a door-opener and walk-inner. Leonard looked up from a plaster model he was doing and gestured upstairs with a putty knife, and I walked up the twisty staircase leaning on the wall.

Okay straighten up and fly right but still look like you've been having the right amount of fun after exams I said, I think silently, in front of the door, and I knocked louder than I expected.

I was easy with the beer, so what the hell could happen, I opened the door and walked in. There were lights on everywhere and Andrea was lying flat on her back on the bed. All she had on was two pieces of underwear and she was staring straight up at the ceiling or through. She didn't even turn her head when I came in. It was a while and she blinked her eyes, and that made me utterly happy.

"Hi, it's me, Bob," I said, standing still.

The lights were bright, all over the room, five or six of them, plugged in on extension cords and resting on every piece of furniture in the room. She was pink and white, her thighs strong and curving forward and joining symmetrical at a pink frilly triangle.

"What's the matter, honey?" I came close to her, slowly, and I heard the hum of the tape recorder, but the wheels weren't turning, there was just an energy hum and the green light on.

I wanted to lie on her and warm her back to life and cover up my eyes till she started moving under me. I sat on the edge of the bed and looked down at her. After a while I put my hand over her fingers on the bed covers and talked to her quietly. It was a long time, but at last she turned her eyes to me and looked at me as if I was the warden come to see how Andrea was today, any better? I raised her hand and kissed the backs of her fingers.

"I love you," I said, at the same time drunkenly realizing that was no health-giving incantation.

She smiled the awfullest smile I've ever seen.

"What's wrong, darling?" I said, and it was awful to say.

"I've been thinking about my father," she said, every word so small I strained to hear.

"I do that sometimes too. I've got two of them, but neither one does me much good," I said, brushing her hair back from her forehead.

Impatient with my hand, she started moving, brushing her hair back and sitting up on the bed. She gestured and I handed her her stockings from where they were hanging in a wisp across a chair back. She knew what I was doing, watching her put them on. I love that moment of a woman with nice long legs, sitting with one extended, drawing the stocking on in a smooth moving of hands and a little reach of hips and thighs. She did the second one slower, and I reached out like a baby with clumsy hand and touched her thigh slightly. She finished with the stockings and I was excited. I bent forward and kissed her leg, pushing my face into the softness of her thigh, moving and prodding with my nose, around to the inside, and my hand on her ankle. Her hands rested for a moment on the back of my head, in my long hair. Then she turned in a large fleshy movement and sat on the edge of the bed, facing away from me. I stretched out on the bed and watched her dress herself. When she leaned forward to pick up her skirt her breasts hung heavily, swinging slightly. I started to ache a little, pleasantly, with alarm.

But she got dressed and I lit a cigarette, watching her touch up her face. She didn't wear much make-up, that was part of her, part of the reason I loved her too, I imagine.

"You worried me badly when I came in. I thought you were dead for a while," I said.

"Sometimes I am, some time I will be," she said calmly.

This made me nervous, because it sounded coffee-club phony and forebodingly true at the same time. I was finding out all the time that the things that sound phony are true for some people. She often made me nervous just that way, nervous and more in love.

There was no time for contemplation, though I knew I needed to think hard, off on the thought that I was going deeper into unknown territory, maybe doing nobody any good, maybe hurting and killing two people or more in the blindness of my days now. But instinct is the man's last resource, and heavier, more trusted because it is his last. Instinct and love. And I loved Andrea now, this was my instinct. I thought of the dark fabric that surrounds us all, that makes us unknown to each other as we pass around foreign and isolate, bodies every day. I thought back to idle moments when I had thought a man was deprived in his life because there were so many people, so many lives he would never know, never have time to know, many interesting lives working out in countless daily gestures that needed chronicling and sheer looking at every minute of the day, all the life. In Morocco and right here. They had to be lopped off for concentration on the known, half-known, the accessible and familiar and special lives of the ones whose circles cut into our own deeply or tangentially. You have to give up the other, because the task, the duty to know even one person other than yourself was too awesome for one lifetime. You were futility and you had to recognize this and ignore it because you cannot give up something you have given up something else for, you can't give up the last thing left to you, left with that last resource, intuition. Intuition fortified with love.

She was staring right into my face.

"Andrea, I came to ask you if you'd eat with me. You will, won't you?" I said, standing weakly with a desire to sit under the weight on me.

Now I was not drunk, I was tired, drained. I needed her very much now, and I had thought it was Andrea who needed me.

Yes she said she would, and she started putting on shoes and things. I watched her step up into high heels. One day I would see her in nothing but high heels and stockings, walking toward me....

Leonard was playing his guitar downstairs. Sometimes he would sit playing his guitar and staring at a half-finished piece of sculpture he was working on.

"I was thinking, why can't there be a trial death?" said Andrea, stopping our walk to the door. Whenever she thought of something interesting she would stop walking and stare at me hard.

"I don't get you, what do you mean, a try-out, and maybe you will want a refund?"

"Bobby, it don't cost anything. I mean, whoever, you know, it could have been arranged just as easy to have death on a trial basis. Sometimes you think you'd like it, but there should be a safety factor. You could have just one test, the second time would be for keeps."

"I'll let you in on my view," I said, trying not to be too light, but I was weak and hungry. "It ain't much of a kick."

"For the bereaved survivors, too," she continued. "I remember at a boy's funeral, it was so final, the worst thing is thinking you'd like to have another chance to do something, and you usually can't think then what it is you would do if you had that chance. But it's too final, for the people left over." Then she said, stating a fact, "You don't know what I'm talking about."

"Yes I do," I said, putting my going out arm around her back. "I've been at funerals too."

She held back still against my arm.

"Bobby, I've been thinking about the tape recorder, and I've changed my mind. There's something on it now, what I was saying a little while, an hour ago. You can listen to it tomorrow if you like, when I'm at work. You don't have to. I'm not going to discuss it with you afterward. That's my one condition, okay?"

"Okay."

I'd forgotten all about Delsing. When we got back to the car he was sleeping with his head pushed grotesquely flat against the side window. The car smelled of stale beer breathing. We woke him as gently as we could, and he shifted to the back seat and rode quietly all the way.

CHAPTER FOURTEEN

ON:

THE MIDDLE CLASSES think the police are lawful protectors of society... the lower class and the intellectuals are together in knowing better... I remember my mother trying to give tea and cake to the police when they came about my father back home, I was sent upstairs but I watched through my secret hole in the ceiling and I know there was something terrible going on that was worse because Dad wasn't home to speak for himself... I knew better than to talk to cops because they were the enemies, yellow-legs in our town, either learning this by heredity or osmosis or the little inflections in my father's random talking, and seeing my mother fawning and commiserating with them made me ashamed of her, more ashamed than I ever would be about what was supposed to be the important and secret part...

I'm going to tell all this, and I'm not going to make any concessions to credibility or explicitness or organization, because if you want you can always turn the machine off... in now and then and no order, just the way it comes to me... whether I've already told my doctor at twenty-five dollars a session or not... you said you're not my doctor, I'll just consider you the inside of this machine, you consider the inside of mine, get it?... and I will not discuss this afterward, you'll have to be satisfied with what you hear here, or there's the off switch...

Where, then...with my father it must have started a long time before I was born, all this Freud stuff, was I a happy child, were my father and mother competing for my affection, did I have to do all my own toilet training...did he walk around my room with his weenie out when I was a baby...you've heard that, you've read it, anyway...say before I was born anyway, when he was alone with my mother-to-be, and that must have been a strange copula verb, eh? Daddy-O, with the accent on the O, being a cipher and a rectum image, so you can see why I am saying this on tape, I can't say it straight at you, not because I'm shy or I think you are too innocent and bumpkinish, it is that I am just too tired of it to organize the way you are expected to do in conversation, and I can't answer questions, this way you can imagine I am an arty radio show like on CBC Sunday night, and consider that the arty-farty stuff you miss in the rush is the intellectual surmise you are supposed to make and pretend you get it all, like college girls do in Cocteau movies...

I didn't find out till a lot later that one of the reasons was that my mother had been taught somehow by her mother that it was debilitating and immoral to sub*mit* to a husband except when you are intending and have prayed to conceive...digest that, and proceed...though of course once in a while, and much to her shame and later blaming it on him, I imagine, she would feel the itch in her own gonads and defensively demand his presence on top of her, for which he would pay a long time, and for which she would offer up self-justifications in the form of prayers...once I slept with a boy who mumbled for what we are about to receive may the Lord make us truly thankful Amen, before he picked up the corner of the sheet...I never did tell my doctor that one...but I told him about my loving mother, every time she did it it was either a pragmatic effort to make a baby or a plain necessary screw, it was never a giving and receiving of love or affection or even mutual biological need, it was never the giving of the best thing a girl can give a man who is nice to her...if she could hear me talking now she would say the devil has got into me, and I would ask her in return if he had ever been fast enough to get into her, and she would start wailing against the robin's-egg-blue dining-room wall...

Or as it says here...

> *I have walked and prayed for this young child an hour*
> *And heard the sea-wind scream upon the tower*

...though she wouldn't be caught dead in this tower, it's the wrong colour, and Leonard would be downstairs...anyway this is the way my father was forced to live, and also asking friends if they would keep his wine for him over at their house because she always poured it down the kitchen sink and said she was saving him from himself...you will only do it to me when I want pregnancy, she said, and that is what I was in her mind, a pregnancy, not a little girl, which I fooled her in because that is something I never was anyway, and me and my father fooled her too, because I was the first pregnancy she didn't want, and she let me know this often enough, pretending she didn't do anything but laugh at her bad luck...and little Bobby, years later was what happened the one time in her life she got drunk and a little human...

But to my father she would say you are not going to come to me with one of those things on you just to satisfy your own greedy lusts, you are not going to make me a partner in your weakening condition and your rotting godless debauchery, as if my father was trying to enter her with a spearheaded tail and a design to topple the hierarchy of heaven into the abyss along with him...anyway I also learned and knew anyway that my father did not have the guts or the morality to go to other women, at least not regularly, and if he had tried that in the beginning, he had given up on it, which when I was old enough

I knew to be true to his character, this man who would not be so rude as to inform a cashier that she had short-changed him by a dollar in a fifty-cent purchase...and which I learned forever one time when I burst into the unlocked bathroom and found him over the toilet, looking at me in that suddenly stopped moment with eyes of a little boy about to be punished for something he didn't understand yet...

I didn't expect it would be so, but I was closer to him after that...

And I then knew that this had something to do with our leaving home for the city, and the reason he wasn't a radio announcer any more, or much of anything else for that matter, except the bread truck he drove one week out of four, poor salesman on piece work, too shy and unwilling to force Chinese grocery store owners to buy loaves of factory bread and half-dozen packages of cinnamon rolls...the first arrest of his life on a mistaken and malicious accusation of homosexual aggressiveness, the young announcer who accused him taking his job after he was thrown in jail, and my mother acting as if she believed it, and saw it as cause of their troubled relationship while he ingratiatingly declined to tell her it was the most important after-effect...

And after he came out of the jail, after we got him out he had no job and no standing in the community, which is a tag for a kind of racial and tribal guilt complex, we had to move, of course, because she said we did, all the time whining that she didn't want to go but he had forced it on us, and it was all because he couldn't control the animal impulse toward depravity in his own loins...she always used biblical language to give force and authority and dignity to her accusations...afterwards he was always scorned or ignored or tolerated by her, as she walked around the house and talked to everyone as if he wasn't there, doing less cooking all the time, and spending most of her day away from home, with God knows what old ladies of the neighbourhood planning other ways to kill us all off...looking amusedly as he cooked the meals for himself and for me, because somebody had to do it, and because he had little else to do now, my mother she was, I had to convince myself, she was looking amusedly at him bending over the stove, and saying at least to herself, but so we wouldn't miss the fun, I guess that is a job he should be doing, him and his new-found romance-life...

I thought if he was just dying of something biological and was wasting in bed and begging me to help him out of the world, I could kill him with mercy, actually thinking of this sometimes, and partly to cheat her out of some of her anticipated years of self-pity and indulgence...I even thought of whether I would keep the mercy a secret from her, just letting her find the body and sitting silently watching her as she wavered about whether she should suspect me, or maybe not suspecting me at all, and wondering what she would do if she knew...

Now you don't have to listen to this if you don't want, and I am always advising you not to, but you suggested it, and I am doing it for me, not for you primarily...

But there was one time I have to put in here to keep on the theme, so to speak, that is about my father if that's what you want to call him, because I swear he was an accidental sire like my dog once snuck off for a weekend and spread puppies all over town before anyone thought to lock up their bitches... which would be a good idea, eh?...anyway this time it was him who came in on me in the bathroom, because we just didn't bother fixing the lock, and there I was putting up my hair which was long then, my arms up and my hands together in back of my head, and my front was sticking out of course... and he didn't back out shamefaced or anything, just came on in, closing the door quietly behind him, and came closer, not saying anything but with a sad look on his face looking at me, at them...and I didn't move either, just stood there with my hands in my hair and nothing on except my little pink panties with the loose elastic...and he was gentle almost, I could say comforting his little girl daughter, as he put his arms around my shoulders, keeping scary quiet, and then he put his big soft hands on my breasts and his face up against me there and I felt his whole soft body, and it was like a weak thing, almost like I could smell it dying in the air... and that was all, he stayed there for a little while and then he just turned and went out, looking the other way...

After that I always thought that a man should have a woman who can be his mother and wife and daughter all at once, or none of these, just an all-purpose comforter and wailing-wall in between...

:OFF

CHAPTER FIFTEEN

NOW IT WAS summer and Delsing and I were working for Buildings and Grounds at the lonely university in the hot sun with our shirts off, getting layers of dirt and suntan on the top halves of our bodies. We were working hard and soft, one day moving heavy wooden furniture from one hot dusty locked-up building to another, so that I was thinking the strain would debilitate me for the strange nights of love on the beach with Andrea, and the next day we would be leaning on rakes on the lawns around the library.

"This is the right kind of work, you know," I said, leaning hard on my rake in the sun. "Cause you don't have to use your mind, you can work away, building up muscles, and at the same time you can be using the time to advantage, wondering why Milton ever decided to be a poet instead of a greengrocer, and similar pursuits of academic inquiry."

Delsing raked up a leaf and took a rest while I raked up a twig and a gum wrapper.

"You trying to tell me you feel positive about work?" said Delsing, ominous.

"No, not positive, just neutral."

"Well, I'm disappointed in you, Small. Don't you know that you have to protect your negative feeling about work? You've got to hate it. *Hate*! HATE!"

"I'm sorry. I'm ashamed of myself."

"Feeling neutral about work is the first step down the awful path to feeling positive about it, and don't you forget that. Don't ever let me hear about you loving your work, you weak son of a bitch."

He turned his back on me angrily and raked up a cigarette package, fastidiously checking it for cigarettes.

"George," I said cautiously.

"Mmfh?"

"I think I'm pretty serious about Andrea, you know."

"More than you are about food?"

"Look, really. It's so goddam hard to know how to make the right choice, you know, when you're trying to handle things and do the right thing about a girl. It's so damn hard to make the right decision, so you don't screw the both of you up."

"Why don't you ask her what she wants? Besides, you've come to the wrong guy. As you doubtless know I have always gone into an affair a doomed man. I've buggered up everything I've ever had that was any good. No, don't say anything, let me indulge myself, poor piteous creature."

"Oh for Christ sake."

"Okay. But I mean that, too. I can't help you. Just do what you would want you to do if you were the girl. You ain't going to have any easy time of it with her, that's all I can tell you for sure."

"Yesterday I came up to her place and she was sitting on the windowsill, looking down at the ground from her turret. She wouldn't move to acknowledge my presence for half an hour. I had to just sit there smoking cigarettes. She could have just slipped out and disappeared from the window frame while my head was down getting a cigarette lit."

"Well..."

"And then she turned around and came in and talked about something else while she got changed from the beach."

"Small, did you ever stop to think maybe she was just looking out the window? God, at home sometimes I would stand there in the front lawn looking up at the mountain and digging the mountain, and my sister or someone would start itching to call the boys from the loony bin. Your ginch writes poetry, Small. She paints pictures. Maybe she was looking at things the way not enough people do."

"Yeah, and later she was digging the beach like hell. Not the way you always do, galloping up and down the sand hollering look at the inscape. She walked up to it cautious as if the water was going to come up and grab her and pull her under and rape her under there."

"Okay, proceed."

"Just a little thing. She said her ex-boyfriend drowned there some time while she was laughing on the beach."

He stopped his efforts to rake up a leaf, and leaned hard on his rake.

"Naturally you asked her to explain," he said.

"No I didn't. And you wouldn't have either, if you had got a look at her face then."

"So you dropped it."

"So I dropped it. We went swimming, or at least I did. She just walked in up to her knees and hollered at me to come back to shore. So I came back and we went home and ate, or at least I ate."

"I'm convinced," he said, raking steadily now.

"What?"

"You've got a problem."

CHAPTER SIXTEEN

SHE WALKED OVER while she was waiting, and looked down from the window in the corner. It was down twelve storeys to the street, to this the six-street intersection, a strange sight from above. There was absolute human order and human trust. The toy manipulated cars moved as if they were on tracks, along lines of convention, agreement. Order. She watched for a long time and none of the cars crashed, none even faltered in their paths, waiting and accommodating one another, the cars came together from six directions, interstitched and moved away again, continuous flow inward and outward. The pedestrians were never run over, they were accommodated. A small bomb dropped in the middle would blow everything outward, evenly. A body dropping in the middle would jam the whole moving machine.

In her dream it was the inside of the car, and they were driving over a long swooping mountain road somewhere it must have been in the Rocky Mountains late at night with the snow drifting across the headlights and the car radio picking up a faraway music station. The heater was on in the car and it was all warm and dozy. Her father was wearing a leather sort of calfskin jacket with fleece turned back at the neck, light brown leather gloves turning the wheel confidently in the turning snowy road. Outside she could see only the snow-flecked light beams poking ahead of them and lighting up fleeting areas of thick snow.

There was no sound but the radio music and it went away after a while. She fixed on the strength of her father's hands on the wheel, holding and turning.

Till they were miles and miles further, she was smoking a cigarette of no taste, and she finished it and reached over to squash it in the ashtray. Her hand fell to his arm, and she felt his arm under the soft leather. She touched her hands over the leather gloves, and worked her fingers inside to the skin of his wrist. The car was stopped and they were holding each other, holding, kissing, and the car was moving along the road with no one driving, his lips at last soft and hard on hers. The snow piled up on the windshield and they went down, down. I've waited so long, I've waited so long, she said, and later she slept. And when she woke she was in her room in Vancouver and it was dark outside.

"Miss, your package is going to have to go to Ottawa. Give us your address and phone number. We'll notify you when we have any word," said the little pin-stripe man behind the long cold counter.

"Would you tell me something?" she asked, coming back from the window.

"Certainly, if I can," said pin-stripe, busily stacking papers.

"Why is the Canadian government so afraid of books getting into the country?"

"I'm sorry, miss. We're just as unhappy about the situation as you are," said the little man, looking her over as if trying to find the physical signs of depravity.

"I'm sorry if I gave you any trouble," she said, turning to leave.

When she got to the street a cold wind was blowing up from the ocean and the rush-hour traffic was crowding south up Burrard Street.

Everything worked from a pattern. A bomb dropped in the middle would clear things outward.

CHAPTER SEVENTEEN

DELSING AND I were grinding through the summer, picking away each day as it hung before us. At night we were often drinking, and it seemed as if this had been the pattern for a long time, a drab day of work followed by a night of beer followed by another drab day of work. On weekends I would see Andrea or I wouldn't. There was no phone in her house and there was no way of reaching her during the week. I didn't even know where she was during the week, working at the neighbourhood house, maybe walking along the Stanley Park seawall, maybe hanging by her fingers on the middle span of the Lions Gate Bridge. Maybe a lot of things, that crazy girl. This I always had to stop myself from saying in fun when I was with her, which was about one Saturday night out of two. I would get into my little car and point it out on Broadway and wonder where we were going, what was going to be at the end, a goony knight errant of the centre lane. Sometimes I would stop in front of her place and run up the fire escape and in, and Leonard would spread clay-sticky fingers and say they hadn't seen her for two days and they didn't know when they would, and I would make little whimpers like Lou Costello and back out with my cheeks puffed up, and I would drive back to the apartment and wait till Delsing was finished working on his play or novel or plain fooling around, and we would drive downtown hooting it up and getting me out of my mood, Dels rubbing his hands and slavering and hollering: "Three miles to the booze belt! Hoo boy! Dames, beers, peanuts and newspapers! Peddlers of stolen watches! War amputees! Drunken sailors with ugly girls walking to apartments!" and things like that, and I would warm up with a couple beers in my belly, and we would wind up on Main Street with Delsing dangerously looking for the cop that beat me up, and me holding him back, drunk as I was...

Or sometimes she would be there, and she would come running out to my car hollering "Bobby!" as if I've been away to Florida and back, and she would jump into the car and kiss me all over, and take a cigarette out of my pocket and say where are we going and say we're going to drink beer down United States of America way at a roadhouse that's where. I would fill the car up with two dollars of gas and we would go, me wondering why she was so excited, not having seen her for two weeks, she could have been across the country and back for all I knew.

"Where you been the last two weeks, what you been doing, ah um" I would say, desperately trying to light a cigarette and driving down the bending road at sixty miles an hour which was tough on the little old heap, but she loved driving that way, made the road thinner she said.

"Been, Bobby? I have been working at the neighbourhood house and dreaming horrible dreams and eating fish and chips at the cheapest restaurant in town, and reading Albert Camus," she would say, and give me a cigarette.

So the hell, we would get pleasantly drunk and dance and play the pinball machines and drive back north, and park by the ocean for a while and go wading and go home and make love for the first time in two weeks. All the time I had rhythmic questions in my mind, but I never tried more than once to ask them out loud, because probably she would explode or brood or get out of the car and walk when I stopped for a red light twenty miles from home, which she did early in the summer, and I drove round and round never finding her then for three weeks.

When we made love I forgot the questions anyway, even forgot the tape recorder that sat beside the bed on the floor, a reel of tape halfway unwound, stuck in mid-speech. Because when we made love with the cool summer night air coming in the window and across us, we were deep lovers who met here every night and went shopping together in the day. She whispered in my ear and I heard and whispered with a breaking voice back, and slept there all night till six in the morning, when I would walk out on the empty streets of Vancouver, up Granville Street and down it, hearing the great echo of a cop's boots two blocks down where the night before you couldn't hear a man talking to you two feet away. I would then take a tremendous long walk down to the docks, maybe west on Pender Street to Ebbe's loft over the painter studio and wake everyone up with hot pancakes for breakfast Sunday seven in the morning, or maybe I would walk in deserted Stanley Park, climb up on the huge log suspended across the road ten feet high, Lumberman's Arch, and look out at misty sea where the gulls would be waking up in their own funny way, flying in easy little loops and squawking out at the foggy bay, and I would sit there having a good-tasting cigarette and imagining soft fluffy Andrea flaked out in satiated sleep piled high with sheets and eiderdown quilts. So thinking I would make a little shiver and pull my jacket collar up tight and walk along the seawall with my hands in my pockets and the cigarette sticking out of my mouth, all alone in the steamy cold park early Sunday morning, see a little horse at the kids' zoo trying to get the morning stillness out of his legs, staring at the ground with bleary Sunday morning eyes, and he would have a couple hundred little scared kids riding him round and round this afternoon, now he's trying to recuperate from a tough night of sleeping, and me too, feeling the light-headed good feeling you have after you've been awake all night and you are all alone where nobody can take anything away from you.

And later, around noon, I would go back to her place and maybe she would be there and maybe she wouldn't, in which case I would go and see someone or maybe I would drive around or I would go home.

One time we had lots of weekend money because Delsing got a cheque from somewhere and paid me off a loan I'd forgotten, so we took off Saturday night down to the Island ferry place and got on the round-bellied boat to Vancouver Island, creaking old ferryboat with cars heavy in its belly and seagulls swooping all around it, diving for pieces of food thrown on the water, Bible birds in a way. Naturally she has a book like Strindberg on her and she wants to be very intellectual sitting in the lounge smoking and reading with occasional quiet prolonged looks out the window into the dark sea night, but I have never been on a boat to the Island before and I immediately set off to roam and explore the whole nautical thing, see lockers and lifeboats and coils of rope, B decks and C decks and axes in glass cases, big painted pipes full of water angling over GENTLEMEN doors to somewhere, old magazine and chocolate bar counter with unbelievable short old purple-haired woman behind it reading Batman comics, spitoons in the lounge, brass and shiny things all over, occasional shudders as the boat turns and tacks wriggling out of Vancouver harbour into the invisible sea. I walked around the thing four or five times, seeing all kinds of funny people settling for the usual two and a half hour run they did every weekend, a bunch of businessmen with cigars and telling giggly jokes and putting arms across backs to help each other into the dining room for mug-up they said knowledgeably, and the short little seaman deadheading this trip. Why are all the workmen of the sea such little short stocky guys with funny clothes they don't mind wearing, purple old goof hats with flaps down, dumb gum-boots, fuzzy wool jackets, army and navy poorman thick pants, suspenders with CANADA written up the straps? Whole thing goofy.

It was almost dark out and I stood at the railing, spitting down at the water where the prow of the boat was making it go slap slap and away the islands were slipping by, often seen several times a day but never settled, likely hiding tribes of hostile Indians and descendants of shipwrecked Spaniards, crazy people on the beach waving frantically at passing scheduled ships every day for the past two hundred years, well I couldn't do anything about it, let them wait for another hundred years. I decided I would go back and find Andrea.

Me being from up-country, the water out there was a good thing for me, and I was thinking of the dead sleep where we could go down to a watery death as in a ballad, but I had been around the boat a few times and I knew all about it now, I knew where to find lifejackets, and I walked through the passageways toward Andrea's lounge, a sea-hardened veteran of many a choppy crossing. But she wasn't there. It was the right place because the ashtray was full of filtertip cigarette butts and her drawing of a funny face was on the steam of the black window.

She was always doing things like that. I didn't know if I'd see her again for hours or days, always ducking out of cafés or my car or away from home for days and never telling me where she'd been. And I always stood there a minute with my feet flat on the floor and something rushing down out of me, slowly flowing down and out of me, giddy in my weakness, and then I would get gloomful pictures of the future, thereupon hollering I don't care, and taking off somewhere, to a park or somewhere. So I started looking around for her, up and down steps and along narrow passageways, peering into rooms and around corners. I made inquiry of an old man who was sitting on a wooden curve-bottom hard dark bench under a fire axe on the wall. Nope, he said, no girl he'd seen, and he stayed here on this bench all night every night. —What, every night?—Yeah, sonny, every night of the year, Nanaimo and Vancouver, sorry I ain't seen your girl, sonny.

And naturally where I found her was way up front on the bottom deck, past the restraining ropes and out over the coils and boxes and tarpaulins and bumps and nautical gear cluttering underfoot, out where you are not supposed to go, right out on the mammoth rising prow of the squat big boat, the dark sea spray banging against the front of the thing, Andrea holding on easily as in the saddle as the rail under her rose several feet in a swoop then down. I stood there, because she didn't know I was around, and I wanted to get finished and climb down and come back, and then I would grab hold of her and ease her back inside to the lounge and we would sit down, me between her and the door. There was a little light coming from somewhere on the ship, so I could see her head, medium short brown hair wet and plastered on the back of her head, she was looking out frontward and down, not now with the fear of the sea, not with the drawing back as at the beach, but interested, it seemed, absorbed in the sea, and she leaned forward and down toward it.

I stood there for a long time watching her, and the dark was filled with cold rain or sea spray. I wanted a cigarette but I knew you couldn't make one out there, and I didn't want the flare of fire in my face, because I didn't want to be blinded from seeing her on her perch for even a second or two. I was afraid I would look up again and see just rail there. She leaned forward, far forward and almost losing her balance.

"Andrea!" I shouted.

She turned her head and looked at me and laughed. I couldn't hear her, but I could see the flash of light on her teeth and the wet plastered hair across her forehead, little gamin. After a while she climbed casually down and came back, picking her way among the boxes and bumps, and she stood beside me, wet and little with no shoes on.

"Hug me," she said.

"Pooh, you're all wet. Where's your shoes?"

"I heaved them in the water," she said casually. "I thought if I heave my shoes in the water I'll have decided something I can't go back on, you know, silly whim. When I was a little child, I used to say if the candle blows out before I can close the window I'll die."

"Dumb broad. What're you doing up here?"

"I always read Conrad in the bathtub; it gives me a certain enamel sense of the open sea."

"You sound like Delsing."

"Thank you, sire. Once I was up at the customs office, and I looked out and lo, we were on the twelfth floor and I saw the street intersection and everything was man-made orderly and I could have dropped like a bomb in the middle, disrupting everything. I can put myself on people and confuse their lives. The sea, though, is an order unto itself, if you throw yourself on it it will swallow you without a ripple. No consternation at sea. Only for those on the beach. Let's go in and get dry."

Which we did.

"We're cut off from everyone out here, Bobby," she said. "Like the space traveller who has to spend two years getting to Venus and back. What if he came back all triumphant and found the world all blackened like hell from an atomic war, and nowhere to go?

"Maybe Vancouver won't be there when we go back," I offered.

"Burnt out, the whole mess. Am I talking strange tonight?"

"A little."

"You'll get the impression I'm a phony black-stocking girl. I don't like those black stockings those art school girls wear. You know they smell around the crotch after a few days?"

"Never smelt."

"Give me a cigarette. God, you're an invigorating conversationalist!"

"I'll admit I have a little trouble keeping up," I said.

"Light my cigarette, and I'll tell you a little story about a man who died with his boots on. My father told it to me. It happened to a friend of his, he said, and it could have happened to him. Maybe it did, the stupid bastard."

"Filial girl, you," I said, lighting her cigarette.

"Once there were a bunch of men working in a logging camp during the depression. It was one fine day at the logging camp and the men were finished work for the day, and they were drying their socks at a little fire they built near the bottom of a sluice run. All of them, that is, except one young logger, let us call him

Charlie. Charlie was just standing there picking a sliver out of his hand and getting a little warm from the fire. Along came a logging truck really fast around the corner and it couldn't make the turn and skidded off the side of the road. And just then the chain snapped on the truck and all the logs came rolling off, right at the group of men, who immediately started getting out of the way. When all was said and done my father was lying on the side of the road with a broken arm, shouting for help, and all the men came and started helping him, tearing his shirt off and trying to ease his arm and all. And it wasn't for a long time that they happened to look back at the fire and there was Charlie lying there with a big log four feet thick across his back, and his long boots in the fire. He was dead and his greasy boots were burning wildly, like yule logs in the fireplace. My father could never forget that. He was crying for help and all the time Charlie was lying there with his feet in the fire. I always wished my father had never told me about that."

"But Charlie was dead, and your father needed help," I said, wondering what the hell she was thinking about.

"Yes, and it took them a long time to get the log off Charlie. His boots were burnt right off, just a sole of one boot left. Nobody thought of putting the fire out."

"But god damn it, he was dead! Your father wasn't making him any deader."

"If it had been me I couldn't have stood myself either, after, and neither could my father, I think. You ask for help from people and you mess somebody else up," she said, smoking her cigarette hard.

"Dead people. People already dead," I said.

"I've had my share of dead people," she said.

It was late at night when we got off the dock. The cop in the waiting room looked suspiciously at Andrea's bare feet. She smiled angelically at him. The whole idea of coming to the Island didn't make any sense, good or bad. And Vancouver wasn't burnt out when we came back.

CHAPTER EIGHTEEN

ON:

WELL, YOU DIDN'T break the tape or throw the machine out the window, and I presume that I am supposed to let this become a routine, the thing we do instead of sex one night a week, and here I can lie on my bed just talking into an ear that is not going to twitch in boredom or whatever, and you can turn the thing off without my ever being any the wiser. So here I am lying on my back on the bed with nothing on, going back, doctor, back to my childhood and the strange sexual rites of the Harrison family, entrepreneurs, gay blades, family of the conjugal weekend around a hearty fire...I call this installment The Orange In The Christmas Stocking...

Because a lot of people have sex as a kind of partnership masturbation, only it is less attentive, and the pleasure spots are not so clearly defined, or that is what they tell me, I wouldn't know, being an accident of the connubial scene myself, the progress report in a program of family planning...though lest I get maudlin, to proceed, to proceed...to start with, I had always thought of God, this is when I was a little kid, I'd always thought of God and dreamed of God as a friendly man who is talking to you reasonably and nicely just before he is ready to punish you. This will hurt me a lot worse than you. Thinking not of my father who could never imagine himself in the position of punisher, no matter what the Freudos tell you, because he was a member of a class called the punishees...so all I had to go on was my mother's statements on morality. Which said that you never trusted anything that gave you pleasure because men and Satan used pleasure-giving as a kind of come-on to sending you down the hurtling path of sin, depravity, pregnancy, frustration, evil singing and dancing, loss of sense about the value of money, you don't know the value of a dollar, she would tell me if I spent the hundredth part of one on a bypassing gum machine, down the hurtling path to a hell at the end, where women could be found drinking and smoking and staying out late nights and lying in bed with men...

It was after that that I was suddenly aware that I couldn't tolerate being close to him in that house, as figured in the scene I always found myself in, we're in the kitchen and me and my mother are working on some housewife chore, each silent from the other, going through it like zombies unaware of each other as ants when they are doing antpile chores and even walking over one another's bodies on their way carrying big sticks somewhere to build some more of the house, so that if I was carrying a dish like a bowl somewhere to put it in the cupboard and she was awkwardly in the way, we would do an exasperated kind of dry groaning and step around each other, hating each other at close quarters and giving none...you know, and he would be there all the time, quiet slunk in a corner sitting at the kitchen table eating an apple from the box downstairs, and I would sit down to polish the silverware and he would be sitting there saying nothing, reading nothing, just sitting there staring in one direction at a point like the handle on the stove lid, eating that apple, so that you were conscious of the absolute presence of his brain more than his body, and that brain was worse than the depraved and broken body...eating that apple...

I couldn't stand it, I would try not to hear him, but it would get louder the more I tried...slurp, crunch, slosh, saliva working around in sluices slooshing around teeth and chunk of apple bitten off in great carrunch, slish slosh, deep awful gulping in his throat, abstractedly staring at the stove-lid handle as he sucked violently and my neck skin slithered up from my collar as he struggled in his throat for another greater pain bringing slasloosh grind, teeth knocking together sometimes, huge breaking sharp hard apple breaking crunch and crunch crunch crunch crunch slather slobber, sucking up saliva and apple juice dribbling down the chin from poor mutilated mouthful of apple... and I would look at him, thinking maybe this would make it better and diminishing the awful noise and the tearing and biting at the fraying edges of my nerves, I would see his skinny neck tendons straining out in two white ropes as he contorted his mouth wide open for another bite, the eyes opening and looking to the ceiling in the effort of the moment, carrunch, the face and neck with uneven shaving of the whiskers black or blue with pieces and clumps of white hair there around the wispy edges of the neck. The apple would be only half gone though he had been crunching and slathering slobbering gulping deep in his throat contorted and painful desperate as if the apple was something in his own bleeding heart a jackal or hyena tearing at himself as I used to wonder what it would be like if a snake started eating at his tail and on up toward his head, if he could not strain his mouth enough maybe it would end with just the head of a snake and a chewed up mangled line of meat-grindered snake flesh, my father eating like that, but the apple was taking too long, I would wish it was over with slather chunk gasp aaahhhwww slurp up dribble from chin and flecks of white apple smidgeons on whisker clump under bottom lip...

The sound getting louder and louder and worse all the time, but my mother simply with her back turned, working away at dishes in the sink, unperturbed, refusing to be perturbed after this long in the arrangement, as you are not disgusted at apes in the zoo with penis hanging out and scratching with long loose easy arms and hands... each crashing gulping bite followed by swirling and slushing of desperate saliva cutting deeper into my nerves, till I would jump up and not look at either of them, it was a conspiracy they entered silently, till I thought my mother knew, till I would jump up and not look, my mother, I thought she knew all that happened between her husband ape and her accidental daughter, and I would leave the room to go to my bed and sit there and smoke a cigarette, with all the time the vision before me of my father sitting on a chair by my bed slurping at the big apple and staring abstractedly at something, the light switch maybe...

At this time many other things bothered me... noses... why don't you turn this machine off and go home... I would stand at the bottom of the escalator in a department store and look at everybody's noses as they came by, you know?... do you know on the whole women's noses don't look any different from men's noses... and most of the noses here except the Chinese and Jap people, most of them are big and prominent and bulgy, English and Russian, German and French noses, long ones that stick way out in front with big boned bridges, I would see streams of people going by on a Friday night, looking right at their noses and they would be going by with their noses out in front of them, as if they were being pulled along by them... and later I would go home, and I have always thought I had a small nose, but I would bend the bathroom mirror doors into an angle and look at my nose from the side, and I'd be surprised how big the goddam thing is, sticking out there, I wanted to pare it down to shape with a potato knife, I wanted to cover it with mufflers and woolen scarves and blankets, paint it an inconsequential colour, walk around with my hand in front of it, or a handkerchief, imagining big bulging blackheads on it, ready to burst and spray the gray white fluid out and embarrass me, as sometimes I would squeeze them in front of a mirror and they would pop all of a sudden and send a line of little white dots on the glass, a surprise as a shot from behind over my shoulder... but there I would be every Friday night shopping for some little excuse and standing by the bottom of the escalator at Hudson's Bay, watching the noses like I sometimes watch hands on a bus...

And there would be all manners of them, like the ones on forty-five-year-old women with dyed hair, large Roman noses with sharp angry bends near the end, hard punishing noses that would quail any man that looked close enough, you'd never notice how crashingly dangerous they look ordinarily, but if you stand there and look at them you see a kind of ominous uncontrolled power in them, noses that could never be caressed or brushed by a tongue, things that could only be handled with tongs and hammers, blunt instruments of destruction and demolition they were themselves... and there are many women who have noses like my mother's, noses that come straight down with no projection down from the forehead, then push out in a button just above the mouth, with round marbles of flesh at the wings, inflating in and out, usually red, with a line of pancake makeup in the crease, and black dots of old pores too many times squeezed out, old tired holes in the pink flesh... these noses are called pugnacious, and they are really bothersome, the kind of thing you expect in your ribs when you are trying to sleep, and I know my father probably fell in love with one of these noses, and detested one for longer, flinching at the ribs when he passed one, without knowing or noticing what it was he was avoiding... noses noses... they say there is something about noses and sex, potency, beware the Hungarian with the long fibril nose...

With our big noses... why don't you turn this off, it's as boring as hell, I am reaching for things to say, to avoid the absurdity of you sitting beside a blank tape, a new art form, procedure as in the Japanese monk facing the wall for twenty years to find his legs atrophied and he became a doll that is pushed over and rolls back upright, that's you sitting there listening to this, Bobby... with our big noses, we have to be careful about the things that get lodged inside them, not only dirt and snot and little black balls of stuff you roll between your fingers and flick away, those things are minute and no more significant than misprints in the daily newspapers...I mean further and more serious things, like pieces of cloth or hair, minute pieces, that you can't account for, you extract a long piece of white sable fur and you try to remember when you had your nose near anything like that, or take for instance other things you are likely to find in a month, depending on the season...apple-blossom petals, under-bed lint, pieces of soup-can labels, squares of glen-check gabardine, tennis-ball fuzz, shavings of swizzle sticks, all yanked out by the inquiring fingernail, we think of so many ways to do ourselves hurt, potato peelings, fudgesicle wrappings, different coloured blackboard-chalk dust, Drano powder, cigarette papers, dried and flecky black shoe polish, baked red paint from fire extinguishers, things we would never expect to find in our own noses, and many things we will never suspect till we are willing to subject our scrapings to a chemical analysis...

Probably the corpses hauled from the bays have odd mixtures of deposits in their noses...if you are still listening, the hell with you...I think too of the things we could use our noses for... the long turned-up bony noses rooting in the ground and plowing great furrows in the back gardens with great snorts of soil to clear the passages of air, the thin delicate noses that walk in the fairway crowd and pop balloons, the fat pudgy noses that gather in the air and lift machines to the skies, every nose has a design behind it, behind its colour and its shape and its cargo capacity, they are all specified for certain jobs, like the varied ants, like the people in H.G. Wells moon voyages, great red noses stop traffic and denote fire escapes and whorehouses, long angular green noses droop and point downward to gloomy nightclubs in the basements of side streets, noses with purple streaks and whorls advertise sicknesses of the bowels and bladder, wide-nostriled noses sweep carpets and sloosh along cleaning gutters at lonely four o'clock in downtown lighted and unpeopled Vancouver streets, a division of labour perpetrated by heredity as in the best of genetic utopian societies...and I hate my nose,

and there is no way out except through transmigration of the soul which I haven't got time or energy for, so there is no way for the unsatisfied except to cut it off to spite the face... and my father's gargantuan nose displeased my mother as his horrendous apple slobbering never could, even in the dark...
:OFF

CHAPTER NINETEEN

WHAT WAS I supposed to do? The old-time image Bob Small was that of a raconteur and wit, boulevardier with dames left tousled and wistful from here to there, though it was not true, of course, me being so shy it took me a week to ask a girl to the prom after which week she would have already had a date for a month anyway; though it always appeared if you could believe what Delsing told you about me, that I was a demolisher of broads, but Delsing has a vested interest in romanticizing everything and everyone he knows, because he has a gnawing fear that his circle of activity isn't very interesting and unique, and that is what bothers him, though I don't give a damn; if it is too much trouble making a date and keeping a girl, then it's too much trouble, and I'd rather just go down to a pub by myself and drink away and talk to some old lobster fishermen in French Canadian, or the best I could do. Though there is something inconsistent in the fact that I am always throwing my pride away to girls younger than me, which makes Delsing scoff and scorn me, though he is the same way, just has a greater facility in pretending he's nonchalant about it all. He's had enough humiliating experiences with lovelorn affairs to fill him up for a while.

Then there's me, with the penitent's repeated vows to change his ways, and his repeated plunges into his vice, where the booze addict for instance is seen one day after a sickness never to touch the stuff again, and is quite holy in his weakened and touchsore body, angelic in a way of vast new knowledge about the brink that waits for the careless walking man. And the next day you are amazed to see him beady-eyed like a ravening vulture, on the track of his bottle, completely unaware of his avowal of the day before, comfortable in his accustomed pursuit. You are puzzled because you don't understand how he can shut the other experience out. That is my way with the young girls; I'm an addict.

The night I knew I was hooked on Andrea I had a dream in which I was standing there with my shoulders drooping and my hands loose and hanging and my head fallen down, everything too tired to move, with just enough strength to keep on standing, or maybe it was that I was too weak even to fall down; anyway the only part of me that was operating was my eyes, even my brain was fogging in from the sides, only able to check what my eyes saw, receive it and not even have the energy to acknowledge the reception. While a skinny young guy with straight hair hanging in his face like a moppet you see by the Great Northern tracks in Vancouver bent over a brown mongrel dog and hacked at the back of its neck with a bowie knife. He stood there slumped over hacking away regularly, almost distractedly at the back of the dog's neck, and the dog didn't fight, didn't even object, only stood there resolutely, sinking slowly down with the sword hole between his shoulders slushing blood down his front legs, looking down at the killer's feet with eyes tired like mine. Finally after about thirty awkward strokes with the knife, the dog fell in a heap, dead, without any noise; I could not tell the moment one of those dull slashes finished him—he was still standing in a fashion at one moment and the next he was lying there on the ground beside a cracked and weedy old flight of concrete steps, a brown clump on the ground.

Next the guy picks up a chicken, which I thought in my tired mind was dead, but it might not have been, might have been only quiet and dull like the dog. Suddenly, or at least without my seeing any change, the skinny guy had a pair of scissors in his hand instead of a knife, and he was ready to go to work on the chicken, which he held up by the neck to let the yellow legs hang down. Then with the scissors he started snipping at the hard feet, a toe off one foot, a toe off the other, and so on, working then, up the legs, snipping off half an inch at a time, very attentively, watching the changing shortness of the legs. Until each yellow stalk was about an inch long. Then he threw the carcass, if that is what it was, over his shoulder, and approached me slowly, distractedly. And I knew he had to have, did have, a weapon in his hands, something bladed and big enough to be in proportion to the knife as I was to the dog. But dark, and unknown, only feared and suspected. So I made a hard effort to turn and run, dreamy and transfixed as I was, and in the striving, I woke up. It was eight at night. I phoned Andrea but the line was busy. Ever since she had got the phone, the line had been busy. So I decided to drive down there without phoning.

But as my little car moved slowly down her crowded street, ready to nose into any unexpected parking spot, I saw them getting out of a taxi, Andrea and a well-dressed guy in a light topcoat. He had his arm around her; she was smiling up at him— star-struck lovers caught in a propitious moment for a soft drink ad. I drove on down the street knowing they wouldn't see me, and got to the end of the block, not knowing what I was going to do. So I stopped the car and stared straight ahead, down toward the still water where the sun was spreading out colours on the night-time horizon. A car honked behind me, and I got into low gear and turned to the left. I decided to go and have a hamburger.

AT THE HAMBURGER PLACE I sat hunched over my plate, alone in a group of couples, sensing them beside me, teenage girls and boys eating hamburgers, in the stopping place between places to have fun, before and after dates, or only going there to get away from home. I got a cigarette out easily, neatly, tapped it on my thumbnail like somebody in the movies and put it in the corner of my mouth, hesitating with the match, all neat, all ruminative. I was feeling bad, and my stomach was upset. She was supposed to have a date with me. She wanted me to catch her? She'd skipped out on dates before, or forgotten them likely. Sometimes I'd been able to find her, but she was always alone, and this was the way I imagined her, as an alone girl, whose loneliness I sometimes shared. I'd never imagined her out with some other guy, probably, as that was all I could imagine, some nonentity, some guy from a mould, a guy in a light topcoat.

"Never seen anything like it," I said to the middle-aged little guy I now noticed was beside me at the counter.

"You don't say," he replied, removing the corner of toast he was just about to clamp his teeth on.

"Yes I do. Never seen anything like it."

He looked at me inquiringly as he picked up his spoon and started stirring his coffee for the second time, around six times clockwise, then a shift like a canoe paddle used as a brake, and around six times counter-clockwise. I tilted forward slightly, watching the little swirls and eddies in his mug of light brown coffee. Once in a while I could see a flash of spoon bowl, but usually it was obscured in the depths of the brown, just the handle sticking out, like an oar handle in the muddy water. Around six times clockwise again.

"It ain't even late at night, not the proper time for a tryst."

"You're right, there," said my friend, raising the toast again. I let him bite through it. He left a dainty semicircle.

"Only about nine o'clock. The first shows in the neighbourhood movie houses will just be getting out."

"Yep. You're out of coffee. You get a second cup for nothing here."

"Thanks. Yep, people going home to watch television now. Prime time. I used to watch television all the time. Sit for hours in front of it and look at it all, commercials and everything. Never switch channels. You ever watch?"

It was a nice easy conversation. I forgot about the guy in the light topcoat, mostly.

"Used to have a television," he said. "Went on the blink, so I moved it to the basement. Going to build a rec-room there some day."

Television on the blink.

"Wonderful thing, TV," I said, stirring my coffee in three revolutions.

"Yes, sir."

I watched him picking up the toast crumbs from the plate and putting them in his mouth. He found it was easier to lift the small crumbs if he wet the ends of his fingers. He worked around the plate, picking up the larger crumbs first and working down to the smaller ones. Finally he picked up the plate and wiped it clean of the smallest toast dust, put it on the counter and pushed it away from him.

"Cigarette?" he said, passing his pack.

"Normally no, but I'll smoke a friendly one with you."

We sat there for a while, smoking our cigarettes and finishing our coffee.

"Usually, I'm bowling around this time of night," he said.

"Yeah? I used to bowl a lot," I said. "Started when I was a kid working in the bowling alley back home."

"Where's that, home?"

"Lawrence. Know where it is?"

"Sure. Bowled there once. Was driving through on my holidays. Nice little alleys."

"My father's got a photography studio there."

"Don't remember seeing it. Was only there long enough for a few games. Nice little town."

"I don't like it. Used to," I said.

"Yeah, well, you get used to the city."

"Anyway, I used to be a pinsetter there. There was this real sexy looking school teacher used to be bowling all the time. I used to sit down there and look up her skirt when she was bowling. Couldn't see much, but I always figured I was going to. She rolled a ball so slow I used to see it coming down the gutter, and when it was about halfway down, I'd jump down in the pit and wait for it. Then I'd catch it as it fell off the end of the gutter. And she's still up there at the other end in the final swoosh pose of the follow-through. It was a kind of contempt I guess, her throwing it and me catching all she could throw. Wasn't till later, in bed, with my hand around it, I'd think she was doing the same thing, saying: go ahead look up my skirt, boy, all you'll ever get is a slow-rolling bowling ball."

The guy rolled a mouthful of coffee round and round his closed mouth, looking for toast crumbs between the teeth, and then he summed it up:

"That's life, young fella."

"Yeah," I said, "a slow-rolling bowling ball."

HER LIGHT WAS STILL ON when I got back to her place. I'd left the car parked in a dark alley a block away, after sitting in it quietly and smoking two cigarettes, not so quietly. I was standing on the little lawn outside Leonard's middle-floor pad, looking up, like at my star. Her blinds were down and the light was still on inside. The tower was a cataract-blinded lighthouse, and I was in a little wet dory, foolishly at sea, determined to ride out the waves and the night. So just when I got myself sat down under a lilac bush I looked up and the light was off. Suddenly. I hadn't caught the moment when it went off and I was irked about that. In that moment I might have seen something, a face maybe, poked around the side of the blind. It was wrong, that they—she—should go to bed, without even contacting the world outside her window, which right now was at least me.

Maybe the guy in the light topcoat had gone home while I was in the hamburger stand. It was ten-thirty now. Why would he go home this early? Why would anyone do anything caught in the radiation around Andrea? Why, for instance, sit on the cool grass outside her house?

That is, I could, I told myself, just arrive and knock at her door, past the embarrassment of Leonard if he was home, and be shocked and cause a scene to see the guy now out of his topcoat, a proprietor. Or she wouldn't answer the door, pretend she wasn't home. Or I could phone her, and listen to her excuse maybe about being sick, or listen probably to the dull buzz of the phone ten times before hanging up. But if I went for the phone, he might get away at that precise time. And then if I did see him and her for sure, how would I see her again? Because I would have to. Better to wait. Easier.

About an hour later, or around midnight, I stood up to take a leak around the other side of the lilac bush, and as I was standing up, I got the idea of climbing up there.

"Mind if I stay here tonight?"

"I'll set the alarm for six in the morning and you can leave then," she had said our first night, and I had been inside the blinded window then, and I had thought this was the first good thing for either of us.

So now I wanted to climb up there and listen to them. Maybe I'd hear her winding the clock.

What if someone saw me from the street? That would be funny, being in jail again for burglary. No, that would not be funny. This time I would swing back at the cops.

Halfway up it was easy, and I went slow, a deliberate step or handhold at a time, partly for the stealth, and partly to put the drama or discovery in its proper place, proper pace, climactic order. Up up up up. The old wooden fire escape went up the back of the building, but swerved over to Leonard's upstairs bedroom window, leaving the turret above safety. From then on I would have to hang over the edge. And nobody to hang her golden tresses from the tower, which also meant I didn't belong there. I rested on the fire escape and hunkered down. There would be no one here at least to see me, except maybe another burglar in the next back yard.

And I had to take a shit. An old pattern of mine. Every time I got into something like this, the old sphincter muscle gave out. It also happened every time I got into a library or bookstore. I squeezed as hard as I could, and thought about the connection. Excuse me, lady, I'm just creeping up here in search of a book. Eventually my haunches shuddered, and it was okay again, for a while.

Conscious all this time that this would be an odious adventure. My kind of love. Tell us about your life of romance, Mr. Small. Well, I remember a moonlight night I was squatting on my lady fair's fire escape with a great tremor imminent in my bowels. The lady, woefully unconscious of my travail and splitting heart, was lying asleep in the arms of a light topcoat. Or alone, unheedful of her love grunting with passion a few arm's-reaches from her perfumed bed.

I should have gone home. If I had thought that anyone was watching I would have descended the stairs with grace, and gone for a walk on the beach. But I climbed up.

How I managed to stay quietly on the side of the tower I don't know, but my eyes at last saw my own reflection in the dusty glass of one of her windows. And I listened. At first all I heard was my own heart, beating probably from the exertion. What would it mean? Any sound? There wasn't anything, I thought. I'll go down, this isn't proving anything. Proving?

Maybe I heard a disturbance of the bed. I knew that bed, my body touching it all along my side. No, I hadn't heard anything. Probably not.

My fingers were aching in their awkward hold on the slight windowsill. I had to go back down. And I shouldn't have come up. What did I know? What should I?

I went back down and laid myself down as comfortably as I could in the scraggy grass of the back lawn. The dew was coming now, familiar Vancouver dew, appearing suddenly on everything. Where did it come from? Did it fall from the sky, or exude from everything? Around three in the morning I smoked my last cigarette, and I thought of going for more. But then I might miss him coming out. Were there some maybe forgotten cigarettes in the glove compartment of the car?

Around five in the morning the dawn came, smoky over the land east of the city, the rest of the country in sunlight, and now Vancouver feeling the first light. It was morning. For them inside it was night, sleeping time. I felt as if nobody should be in bed. Footsteps echoed down the street, loud, someone going to work already. Why didn't they wake up? What was wrong with me that I was always goofing around somewhere in the city at dawn?

I walked around to dry up the dew on me. The birds were talking all over that part of the West End. Why didn't birds wake people up? A truck went by, roaring in second gear.

Somebody was going to see me. Maybe Leonard worked in the first light of day. Painters, I told myself reasonably, work with natural light. I decided to take up a better position across the street, where I could watch the other side of the turret.

Delsing: Where have you been all night?
Small: Lying in the grass, waiting for the birds.

I looked at my watch: ten to six. I was dying for a cigarette.

The blind lifted slightly from one corner, and a face looked out. It was the guy with the light topcoat, hair messed up.

I got into the car and drove across the Burrard Street Bridge, going home. But I stopped for coffee and cigarettes at a lonely morning Chinese café. One other guy was there, having fried eggs with ketchup, and playing the jukebox over and over again, loud cowboy music.

I didn't really see the face properly. It was just there a second. I was too sure: it was the guy in the light topcoat, looking to see if the coast was clear. Maybe it was Andrea, looking to see what kind of day it was. Or to see if the coast was clear. Why didn't I know what time she went to work? It was probably Andrea. If I hadn't walked away so soon I would have known for sure. I was scared to actually see him coming out of the house, I made the uncertainty on purpose, so I wouldn't have to make a clear decision. No good going back now. I was nowhere. I'd wasted the whole night.

Delsing: What were you doing lying in the grass?

Small: Degrading myself. Fooling myself.

No, just continuing the old pattern.

CHAPTER TWENTY

THAT NIGHT THE fog stayed in the city instead of crawling away under the cold black sky. The fog stayed. It rolled occasionally, down an empty street by the ocean, the kind of fog that catches a man by the arm and chills him through his clothes over his chest. Cars crept through it, lights low, picking their way home, drivers with cigarettes, trapped in their small chambers with that slight warmth, a cigarette, and the faint glow of the dashboard. It was a night of sudden policemen, strange sounds a block away.

She was home snug in bed, but he was miles away through the fog, in the East End of the city, where the fog was not the fresh fog of wet lawns, but a smudgy kind—it ravelled round people and other figures. He was drinking alone, a cold clammy last beer while the waiters stood around impatiently, going through the nightly ritual of hurrying the customers out into the midnight of Main Street, where there would suddenly be several clusters of drunks along the dim sidewalk, cluster for a few moments, then break away to separate cars, rooms, alleyways.

He walked toward the street where he had left the car, for the first time that night thinking of his wife, his wife, of his daughter, drunk defiance and shame coming in waves like fog. She would be asleep when he got home, grunt obscenely when he dropped his limp body on top of the covers on his side. If he lay on top of the covers it was his doing, his limpness, a thing of design, and in the morning she would not speak to him, while he had his headache and could not open his eyes. She could be wearing a police uniform and he would sleep blissfully. In the afternoon there would be the newspaper.

The other, she knew nothing. Alone with her pointless job and somewhere in the old West End, living with artists...could have got through to her, an ally, or better than that, a mind, to reach, after all these years, a mind. Not something on hinges, shut to your words before you utter them, till eventually you don't bother to intend to utter them, to form them at all, you let her think what she will think, satisfy herself that you are stupid, a man who loses, she the woman who suffered, kept you from destroying yourself, and was somewhat destroyed herself in the process. Was that true? Was he that? Shit, let someone else decide that.

The car was covered with dew, small streams and tributaries of water, cold to the touch. He put his first two fingers to his head, cold, wet, between his eyebrows. Bless me too, father, for I have sinned, and am afraid. The keychain dangling from those fingers clinked against the gold ring on the third finger. He bent and put the key in the door. The fog slipped into the car with him.

(Far across the city she buried herself deeper into the covers and woke for a second, warm in the dark cotton. I shouldn't have said that to him, heaven knows what kind of trouble he'll drag us into, where he is, I should have kept him home where I could watch him at least, the lesser of two evils, how much money did he have with him, well, I don't care this time, I don't give a shit. Finally the covers settled round her neck, and she went back to sleep, her mouth open, a faint light reflecting from her moist teeth.)

The fog outside the window was thick. He moved his car slowly, not sure whether the white line to the left of his wheels divided the lanes on his side or the other. The thing to do was to watch for headlights, watch for lights, steer clear of them, to their right, when you know for sure. He recognized the corner and turned left, forgetting to look for the light—traffic lights always show through any fog, he knew that. He watched for the next one, and saw it move from red to green, then a car horn behind him. He moved on, west, home.

Where she had started it by saying something worse than usual, but she had done that hundreds of times, he was just looking for an excuse, he couldn't remember now what she had said. But it came to him—Andrea. She used that whenever she wanted to finish it. Andrea. But he knew Andrea was what bothered her most, because it had to be a lie when she used Andrea against him, they both knew that, and he knew she knew it. Because of course Andrea hated them both, but hated him in disappointment, frustration, because of what he had become at irretrievable age fifty. Andrea hated her mother twice over, for making that happen, and as a person, she would hate her if she didn't know a tenth of that. As a human being. What a feeble groping for comfort. The fog inside his skull was at least warmer than the one outside, there was at least that comfort. He wanted to go to sleep, before he got home, before that bed.

He was at the other corner now, he could see the bank with its old brown foggy stones. This was where he turned left. He turned right. Down the hill into the deeper fog, colder air. It wasn't time to go home, not yet. The car would nose into that driveway so easy, so familiar, the cloying, alarming familiarity, perverse security. First a drive around this part of town, this part, the part he had found in his first trips to the city, before he was married, his part of town, which he never saw since then, unlovely but alone on a night like this. The CPR tracks, old beer parlour of tug captains in navy-blue toques, big sheds, nails driven half way in, street bending to the contours of the shore and the old buildings, older than the streets.

The familiar old street extended in front of him, into the cold fog. He nosed the car down it now, faster in this old familiarity, the straight street, bumpy under the wheels. The West End was behind his back now, far across the city, as he drove down the long pier, off into the foggy air over the dark cold water, the front of the car dipping already toward the sea.

CHAPTER TWENTY-ONE

I STAYED AWAY FOR a couple of weeks, and I didn't see her at all. A couple times I almost phoned, I even thought of disguising my voice, just to make that contact, to make sure I guess she was still alive. There wasn't anything in the papers about a girl jumping off the Lions Gate Bridge, but that wasn't the way she would do it anyway. She would get into a kayak and paddle north till the ice surrounded her, and then she would lean back and smoke a cigarette till the ashes fell on her frozen chin, something like that. But that's how worried I was, reading the papers, wanting to phone her. But I didn't. And after a while I was surprised to find out I really didn't want to phone. Life was returning to normal, or boring, whatever you want to call it.

"Hey man," said Delsing one night of great smoking and beer drinking. "What's with you? Where's the *joie de vivre*, what's her name? The newest one."

"Don't know," I said.

"Aw, come on fella, let it pour out."

"So you can use it in a story, old friend?"

"Ah shit, forget it," said Delsing. The master of dialogue. He later suggested that we go down to the Georgia pub for college-man beers, and that was all we said. I didn't even want to talk about Andrea. Sometimes, though, the nerve endings around my arms and thighs got that strange doing-nothing feeling. Walking down the street helped.

BUT I WAS UP one night reading the French magazines and smoking bad-tasting cigarettes, the low-key lazy student thing you get once in a while, especially in the summer. There was a loud bang, and I jumped in fright, actually started out of my chair, as the old novels say. Bang again. Like an old novel, again, someone was throwing stones at my window.

It was Andrea, of course. I met her outside, me in my old blue bathrobe over my pyjamas, and mocassins on my feet. I got into her sports car with her, and away we went. And this time she looked like a strange beautiful girl I hadn't seen before, or maybe a long time ago in a James Dean movie, her hair stringy and hanging down beside her ears, no make-up on, just some dirt on her face.

"You look like you just got out of bed," I said, and I was proud of myself for not adding anything mean about whose bed—ugly pride.

She wasn't holding back, and she wasn't coming either. I was holding back, I was after all the affronted party, and that was something I couldn't do, I couldn't just forgive. And it took me a while to be able to look over at her instead of out the windshield for cops. She was driving fast.

"Where'd you get the car?" I asked. At that point I should have taken out a cigarette and lit one for her, one of those little gestures I make with slightly strange acquaintances. But I had come out of the house without cigarettes. I had come out of the house pretty fast. One look out of the window, and I had almost tied myself in knots trying to get the bathrobe on.

"It belongs to a friend of mine," she said, and I waited for more, thinking light topcoat, but I knew also I couldn't push it. It was that old thing, me the fumbler, and her the girl with half her mind in a further world I didn't know anything about. It was like that first time I saw her in the folk singer place. I could look at her and place her from my vast experience and admitted high intelligence. But she had a past that was able to view the world I could only describe with my head full of reading. When she looked out the windshield of the car, she knew there weren't any cops in the way because she had seen everything in one flash, and the car would nose into any close future.

So we got to where she was going, which was of course the water, this time lonely Wreck Beach, which meant we had to get out of the car, into the little forest on the edge of the cliff overlooking the Pacific full of log booms waiting to be pulled up the Fraser River, you could see them on a night like this, the moon shining in a sky of no clouds, silver off the logs disappearing sometimes in a flash that was ocean and moonlight. Then we had to scramble down the clay cliff to the short bit of sand next to the water. They called it Wreck Beach because a ship went under some time, just off where the logs were now. It may still have been there, under the water. That may be where we're going, I thought, and I thought about the pyjamas I was wearing. I would make a peculiar and newsworthy corpse for the morning police and newspapers, stuck in the hold of an old sunk ship, my bathrobe floating above me.

Lying on a smooth old waterlogged log in the moonlight, she looked better, the light gentle on her long exposed throat that looked like sex and death, a Bergman movie sort of light on her neck. Her hair was stringy, but here it made her look as if she had just come out of the water. And I thought, that was possible, too.

"I'm a little cold in my sleeping attire," I said. "You got a cigarette?"

She tossed me a package, which I dropped in the sand, and this completely destroyed any dominance or righteousness I was going to hold over the scene. I bent over and reached around in the gray sand till I found the cigarettes, and lit one for each of us. The matches were inside with the cigarettes. I didn't have to fish around in the sand for them. This was the first time I could remember not liking her, the first time I wasn't entirely a poor captive.

"I quit my job at the neighbourhood house," she said.

"Fine, now I know you quit your job at the neighbourhood house. Do we go home now?"

I didn't really want to talk like that. It was as if I was in some sort of drama, a play, saying things the rigid text laid out. Away in front of my consciousness I knew she was in trouble, or something was troubling her, but there was an insulation there between us, something like the fuzziness of the moonlight, where you could make out shapes but not lines and details. I was wishing I had stopped to bring my glasses.

"Bobby, I came and threw stones at your window."

"And scared the hell out of me."

I smoked the cigarette now, like an unrelenting movie villain. I was glad of the muted light. I was realizing that no matter what, it was me who looked stupid. I wanted to stop posing. Something was wrong with the way I was acting, and I thought it was just being away from her for two weeks.

"I wish I could have said something on the tape recorder and left it with you," she said.

"Yeah, maybe I could just get another tape recorder and put it on *record*. My tape recorder could listen to your tape recorder."

"That's what we're doing, isn't it?"

"Well, look, go ahead and talk. There's nobody here but me and a lot of sand," I said. I sounded cold. Or hurt, not what I wanted. "I'm on *record*," I added.

"I'm sorry, Bobby. My father's dead."

Her eyes were looking straight at me, black holes in her white face. She could have come out of the sea. Her father, what I had heard about her father on the tape recorder, her dream, there was something frightening in those dark eyes.

"I didn't know."

It was all I could say. I had never met her father, just heard about him from her, and from her dream on the tape. I did know it had to mean a lot to her. Something there was, it was something like there was a mistake between her and her mother, Andrea should have been the wife. It had something to do with the way she was with men. The ones that died and the ones she had told me she could like but had to treat badly.

"He drove his car off a pier," she said.

The ocean again. Always the ocean. I felt it behind me, and I suddenly wondered which beach it was that boyfriend of hers had drowned at. Then I thought of the other story she had told me as she hung over the deep ocean on the way to the Islands—that time it was fire. Water and fire. The baptism, the purgatory. My mind was going away into abstractions, and I hated myself right then, my mind was pulling away, I was escaping, from death, or my commitment because I was there with her.

So I went over and sat beside her on the log, and put my arm around her. All I was trying to do was give her something to touch.

"I saw it in the papers," I said. "I just didn't connect it."

"In the papers they said survived by his wife and two children. I'm always surviving. I've been surviving for a week now, Bobby. What have you been doing?"

A little needle of resentment touched me then, I didn't like her trying to make me feel guilty.

"Studying," I said. "And taking long walks."

"Thinking about me?"

"Yes," I said. I didn't say how much.

I had never seen her so defenceless. I had seen her angry, and more characteristically, withdrawn, gone into that strange world of hers that scared me. This was the first time I had seen her this little. She let me hold my arm around her shoulder, but she didn't lean on me.

"Bobby, please kiss me," she said, and it was touched with desperation.

I felt as if I was doing something awkward, but I kissed her, then I stood up in the sand and held her up to me, and kissed her again. But all the time I was thinking, and I could hear the ocean moving among the log booms. I was aware that it was then I would naturally say I love you, but I didn't. I was afraid to say anything, or it would come out like robot language, and she would be aware of it too, I knew that.

Whose sport car, I wondered.

She opened the buttons at the top of my pyjamas and put her face on my chest, her mouth against my skin warm and wet, and her hands reached around me, under the open bathrobe now, at the small of my back, then with deliberation, inside my pyjamas, down on my buttocks, and her mouth was wet on my nipple, and she was leaning on me. Then she slid to her knees in the sand, and her hands pulled my pyjamas down with her. The ocean was gone then, the only sound was a pounding of my heart I had not heard in years.

SHE LET ME OUT of the car, and I leaned in the window to kiss her, then I said goodnight and watched her drive away, to wherever she was going. When I got inside the house I took off my bathrobe and pyjamas, and got naked into bed. I could feel sand on me before I fell asleep.

CHAPTER TWENTY-TWO

THE HARBOUR OF Vancouver opens through a narrow strait of water around the end of Stanley Park, where thick evergreens give the boatsman an illusion of old-time Northwest, Indians in the trees overlooking the tall bluffs with broken rocks in the edge of the water below. Ferries from the Island and big ships for cargo have to circle around the peninsula of Stanley Park on their right, and turn to the right, ease in under the thin green suspension of arcing Lions Gate Bridge, which shoots out from the trees on the Vancouver side, over to the flat factory beach of mud under the swiftly-sloping mountains of the North Shore. Much of the time there is a cold fog obscuring the bridge and the headland, perhaps the tops of the bridge towers show over the gray clouds. Automobile headlights appear smudgy on the bridge. The gulls don't fly then, and it is quiet, except for the occasional foghorn.

She knew what the bridge was at times like that. Stanley Park was a natural place for her on her walks, and the Lions Gate Bridge extended from Stanley Park, on nights like this, it led off only into the fog. All the poets in town wrote poems about the bridge. It was no private thing; or more truthfully, it was a series of private things. No one living in Vancouver could be long unconscious of bridges, especially this one.

The park was empty. There weren't the usual crowds of people at the approach to the bridge. The telescope with the dime slot, aimed at the North Shore mountains, nobody eyed its eye. The foghorn of the lighthouse at the channel entrance sounded every two minutes, but there could have been no ears to hear. A small foreign car suddenly appeared out of the bridge fog, its light showing a second before the wet steel fenders came into sight, and it passed by her, slowly, as if feeling its way into the deeper fog of the tall trees.

She stepped out onto the bridge, and in front of her the fog was not still now—she could see the rounded clouds of it going across in front of her, through areas left between crossed steel of the girders.

Her high heels clanked on the steel of the empty bridge. It was the first time she had worn these high heels for months. On the wet bridge they felt as if they would slip under her. She leaned against the tubular rail and tried to light a cigarette in the wet windy air. With her last match she managed to get a corner of it lit, and she pulled hard on it, watching the burning part creep up one side, till it was well lit. She dropped the empty match folder over the side, and it flipped out of sight.

On she walked, trying to get the sense of the climb, the slight bow the bridge took till its highest point halfway across. She wanted to know when she was at the middle. If she concentrated it seemed as if she could feel the thing rising. The water was far below, and it would be dark and big waves, coming in with the tide.

> *Society is all but rude,*
> *To this delicious solitude.*

The sea is also a garden, someone said. It was some poet. The sea is also a garden, untended, a place of further solitude even unspoiled by anyone who walks that way. I sing in my chains like the sea, another one said.

She arrived at the middle of the bridge, the highest part, farthest from the water. Now it isn't the sea, it is the water, she thought. She leaned against the tubular rail and looked into the fog, face toward the city side. In there, in the city, many things happening. Man dying in his own saliva in his own room all alone, or in a back room off a party. Man suffering coronary thrombosis at the fag-end of life, action far behind him. Man finally dead after filling his veins with whisky for all his adult life. Man dead of another stroke, lying in state in the slumber room at one of the smooth quiet funeral homes with coloured night lights in front on the lawn. What kind of home is that, a funeral home? What do you do, to come home to a place like that? The same people sponsor all the religious shows on television, these home bodies. They tell you the spirit is flown, the body is only earthly, returns to the earth. You pay a thousand dollars a foot for the earth, and your spirit is flown, leaving somebody to pay the bill. Nation of bill-dodgers. No one has a right to leave a dead body behind him. Give it to the sea.

Give it to the sea. Join nature that way. Join the others who went into the sea. They come and they fish you out again. Into the earth.

She tried to lift her foot over the rail, but it was too high. She put her foot back down, clumsy in the high heels. She thought about throwing these shoes, too, into the dark unseen water. Then she tried to pull herself up to the rail. She got into a sitting position, finally, on top of it, leaning out to look down. All she could see was fog.

A car stopped, and a man got out. The lights had come suddenly, no sound, and then the car was stopped. The man came over and put his arms around her hips and held her.

"I'm holding you okay. Just slip down here," he said.

She slipped down, and her skirt went up and then fell down. At the same time, she came down too—and it was a moment out of time—this little return to solid footing instead of the open air above the water.

"Okay, you're holding me," she said, not looking at him yet. "And who are you?"

"Mike."

"Okay, Mike."

"And who are you, now?" he said.

"It is enough you have me," she said. "So you don't have to have my name, too. You'd better not leave your car just sitting there, someone will smash into it in the fog."

He led her to the car and waited till she got in, then closed her door and went around to his side. They drove on, to West Vancouver.

Once again her skirt had gone up when she got into the small car. She left it that way. Her bare leg went well with the high-heeled shoes. She was surprised to notice she still had her shoes on. So she left her skirt where it was. It didn't matter anyway. It was a moment out of time.

"Light me a cigarette? Have one yourself," he said.

She looked at him as he took the lighted cigarette in the corner of his mouth. He was older than she had thought at first, but he was trying to look younger than he was. He must have been at college ten years ago, with the fraternity boys in Brock Hall. His hair was cut that way. Decidedly not dangerous, not very interesting. But the car was messy inside. That was not too bad. She didn't ask where they were going.

He stopped the car, and that was what it was, his apartment. It was halfway between the water and the mountains, where the oldest buildings were giving way to the new high apartment buildings. He came around and opened her door for her, and she went with him.

CHAPTER TWENTY-THREE

AFTER THE NIGHT at the beach I still kept moving away, not that I didn't want her, it was a part of my brain, pulling me away, like the weighted side of a lawn-bowling ball. Away from her, from the commitment, I think. I didn't want to be responsible for her. But I *did* want to. It was confusing, and I move away when I'm confused.

Andrea. It was still the name that used to go through my brain like a strobe. But now it fell flat when I whispered it experimentally in my room. And the same way, I am having trouble talking about her. I just don't want to, especially now, when it's all over. It was nearly as bad then, but not quite.

I WAS JUST ON my way out of the house, a scarf tied in a knot around my neck, I was going down to the Italian store on the corner for cigarettes. An hour before I knew I was going to need cigarettes, but I decided to wait till they ran out. This way I would have to leave the room and get out, do an errand, get cigarettes. I needed the activity. At the store I would also read the magazines, I would even look at some of the ones I usually didn't even see. It would use up the time.

I was just outside our door when the sports car came up to the sidewalk. She had the top up, and her head was inside, in shadow. I walked round to the other side, and worked my awkward way in, my long legs bending. I could fit my attention to that. She had the car moving before I shut the door.

"I have to get cigarettes," I said.

She handed me a pack. Always the cigarettes, now. They were supposed to be a girl's defence. Now I was using them to occupy myself. I wondered if we were switching roles. We were always using this car that belonged to her friend, now.

"I haven't seen you for a couple days," I said.

"You ain't been looking."

"I been studying," I said.

"Yes."

When I talked with Delsing it came out swiftly, in long sequences of smart-ass dialogue, jokes, poses, postures; characters stepped into for the duration of an argument or a mum show. It had been something like that with her too at first. I had been able to use the deft edge of my tongue, this way of paying homage or something. Now I didn't want to talk, and when I did it was in five-word sentences of dull words, each one thick in my mouth. And she couldn't talk unless I had loosened the conversation. I wanted to get her talking, but I couldn't let my own tongue loose.

So I smoked the cigarette, and watched where she was driving. We were always going somewhere now, not to a place, but to be alone.

She stopped the car this time at a parking lot in Stanley Park, and got out, and started walking into the trees. I followed her, but not as before, now I walked slowly, and she could slow down to let me catch her. Then she disappeared.

I thought I would just walk straight ahead, in under the tall ferns and rotting fir trees. She would reappear and I would let her walk with me.

This was the park I had always returned to when f felt like I had to return. It might have been because of when I lived in Lawrence, where we went to the hills every day in the summer and as often as we could when school was on. This was a different kind of bush, the moist kind of the Coast, the pre-Spanish

West Coast, with large ferns and rotting logs lying on the ground, and big salmonberry bushes a man had to push his way past. It was also in a way a city forest, on the edge of the city, where people kept to the paths marked by signs that told where the bridle path was, where the lake was. I had walked there with a girl once, she was from the city, and she bothered me for talking all the time, and smoking, and butting my cigarette on the leaves on the ground. I wasn't at all respectful of the forest, she said, or I would be quiet and listen, and I might see a squirrel. But she was from the city. Once Delsing had shown me a poem by Gary Snyder about working in the bush in the interior, and that made more sense. He wasn't worshipping the forest, in fact if you said forest it tipped me off. His poem was about a bulldozer knocking down small trees and cracking a rock outcropping, and the noise, and the smoke that broke out of the rock. This girl from the city would have thought the loggers in the "forest" were not communicating with nature. I didn't feel like it, I didn't like feeling as if she owned this place, and the trees were not a cathedral after all. I saw just as many squirrels as anyone.

I don't know what the park meant to Andrea. But I thought it must be something like the ocean, because it was big, she could lose herself in it, and of course this was why we came here. She was losing herself, and she needed someone now to see that she was losing herself. That was a stupid way to think, I told myself. I sat on a very big log and had a cigarette. A cigarette in the bush tastes very good, like the first cigarettes you smoke when you are very young.

One time when I had been working in the forest service in the summer I was out with a crew, marking timber, and the other two thought there was a moose in the area, which was rare, so they went on ahead, and I was to wait there and see if he came from the rear. So I lay very still on the ground, which was a slope, and after a while some small birds came to see what was happening. I stayed so still that they stopped in the trees just over my head.

Then when I didn't move, they came closer, till one of them was just in front of me, on a stump, and looking as if he was going to land on me next. Then I made a slight noise in my throat, and they flew up into the tops of the trees again. They were birds and I was a forestry man, that was good enough for me.

I also remembered that it was here I would come after leaving her house in the early morning, and this made it strange to be here in the park with her. If I was.

I stubbed my cigarette on the old log and left it there with its trade name on it, and started walking again. When I came out of the trees I saw her leaning against the old mossy rail beside the path that went along the edge, above the water. She was looking that way, out to the small wooded islands that lay in the flat water between the mainland and Vancouver Island. I walked up to her and leaned on the rail beside her.

"This is the western edge of the continent," she said.

"In a manner of speaking. There's also the islands," I said.

"I've read that on the western edge people come up against the edge they have in them."

"Oh yeah?"

Now there was something wrong with the way I was talking again. When we first met she stopped me from talking in a theatrical way.

"Vancouver has the highest rates of divorce and suicide in the country. California is like that in the States," she said, looking out to sea.

I looked at her face, and it didn't say suicide, and now I wasn't afraid of her killing herself anymore, at least not as much. Her face said puzzlement, and maybe fear, and she looked out at the ocean as if she was trying to remember the eons ago when she had crawled dripping from it, to become an earth-going creature. She was very beautiful then, in that way that strange-looking girls suddenly become beautiful when you have known them for a long time and you suddenly see them from a new angle. She was looking out to sea, her chin up slightly, like a sailing sloop, and her blouse was open and I could see her white bra. Her hair was straight, and some of it was wet and stuck to her neck.

But I was looking at her as if she was a strange girl, an esthetic experience.

"Well, here we are at the western edge, and now what are we going to do?" I asked.

"Well, I am not going to jump in the water, so don't worry about that," she said, slight derision in her voice.

"Oh, I knew that."

Suddenly she turned and slapped my face hard. It was the kind of slap that would have surprised me enough at one time to bring tears to my eyes, not crying tears, just the physical reaction. This time I was surprised, but no tears came to my eyes.

I didn't put my hand up to my face. I looked at her over the rims of my glasses because they were knocked crooked.

"That hurt quite a bit," I said, and it was as matter-of-fact as hell.

She turned and ran down the path, turning a corner, the red blouse finally disappearing in a maze of branches and ferns. There was no sound of feet left on the damp leaves of the ground.

This old park, I thought, this old park is full of things. Once there had been a famous fat pigeon there with one leg, used to hop around where people were buying hotdogs and popcorn, in competition with the other pigeons, and he was the fattest pigeon in the park. In the shaded slopes off the paths, large green slugs moved slowly from tree to tree, and their paths were silver behind them. On the leafless stumps overlooking the old Spanish seacoast there were great growths of something like mushrooms with no stems. In front of my face as I walked along the path after Andrea hung the inchworms on their invisible strings, they swung back and forth in the breeze, pendulum lost in the middle of the trees on the edge of the city, they marked time at the end of land of the great northern continent. It was a lot of shit to be thinking, but Andrea had run along this path, and I was following at my slow walk. I knew I would catch up with her again.

Long long ago when I had first known her, I would have run headlong down the path, calling her name, on the edge of frenzy. But I had known her an age. There was something wrong with all this, I kept thinking of that. But now I could walk and wait. I had never been like that before. I was moving away, and I could only think it must have been Andrea that made it happen. But that couldn't be true.

I found her in a small clearing. She was leaning on a huge log that came up to her shoulders, and it was burned black where she was against it.

She looked at me with wide eyes as I approached. Then she started yelling.

"How can you just stand there when I slap your face! All this time I do the bitchiest things to you, and you hang your head and say it hurts a little, or you don't say anything, pretend pretend, you pretend it doesn't happen! You pretend all the time! I've seen you all the time! I've seen you all my life. You! Make! Me! Sick!"

She spit in my face after she said that. I didn't even know I was doing anything. My fist hit her in the face, and then she fell on the ground. Her eyes were blank for that moment before she fell. Her mouth was a round black hole. Then she fell straight down on the ground like an empty shirt.

I couldn't have done that. It wasn't me. I didn't bend over. I just stood there, very tall, because she was lying on the ground.

"Daddy, Daddy!" she said, gasping for air. "Daddy, Daddy!"

When she looked up at me there was blood on her bottom lip.

"Please take me home," she said.

As we walked back to the sports car of her friend, she leaned on me, and she held on to my arm. She had never done that before. All I could think of was getting home. I would stop and buy a package of cigarettes at the Italian store on the way.

CHAPTER TWENTY-FOUR

WHAT, THEN, COULD be the matter? Music, the passion of the dance, nonsense on the five tips of every star. What could be the matter? Who ran the world in the olden days, before elevators? How many angels can screw on the point of a needle? Or any of us, for that matter? Why can't a person have colours instead of emotions? Who has jumped off the Lions Gate Bridge and survived?

Andrea, it was, walking through the slight drizzle that came with the dark, thinking of home on the way home. Not the tower with its books. The house in the other part of the West End, with its front room lights turned off in respect for the dead. She finally arrived on the dry front step, and opened the door. Why knock on your own dear home? Her mother was in the kitchen, washing wide panties at the kitchen sink.

"What the hell are you doing here?" the woman at the sink said.

"I guess I just wanted to come and look at you," said Andrea.

"Why didn't you come to the funeral?"

"I didn't want to. There wasn't anyone there I knew."

"There was your father."

"Was."

The woman wrung out the wet panties, and there was corded power in her arms. Andrea looked at the arms, thick and meaty, with loose white flesh hanging behind and above the elbows. Strangling arms.

"You could have come and read a poem. He would have liked that. Why didn't you come and read some enlightening poem about death being the beginning of life? Or have you forgotten that one?"

"You talk so nice, Mother. I can tell you really loved him."

"Oh no!" said the woman. "Oh no, it's you that loved him, in the bathroom, in your bedroom, God knows where else. You have to look other places now for that. Very nice girl I got. You, you're just like him, only this time a woman, and that's worse."

Andrea wanted to do something then. She sat down at the yellow painted kitchen table, and moved her wet raincoat flaps so they wouldn't be on her legs. There were no empty and dirty dishes around, there was no mess on the floors. It was all very neat. Business as usual, a picture home, neat as a pin. Nothing had happened out of the ordinary. The rain came every night, punctually after the stores closed. Her mother walked out of the room and came back with a handful of ashtrays.

"What are you doing?" said Andrea.

"I'm continuing. That's what I'm doing. I'm continuing. I'm certainly not taking a luxury cruise to Hawaii on the insurance money. Is that what you came for? To see what you could get out of the money?"

"No."

"Because you can forget it. If I ever get it—as soon as they find out he didn't kill himself—*if* he didn't—I'll get it all right. He was probably drunk. Being the responsible husband and father, running around the skid row, drunk, and probably worse than that..."

Andrea turned and looked away, at the wallpaper with the pictures of happy teapots.

"...that is, if there were any little boys out that late at night."

"He should have been at home enjoying the cunnubial life, is that what he should have been doing?" said Andrea. Her voice came between shaking lips. Her whole body was shaking in the chair.

It was the inside of the car, and they were driving over a long swooping mountain road somewhere it must have been in the Rocky Mountains late at night with the snow drifting across the headlights and the car radio picking up a faraway music station. The heater was on in the car and it was all warm and dozy...

"...connubial life, what do you know about it? If I ever had a total of ten days connubial..."

Fat mouth. The words drifted back and forth, loud inside the head then off somewhere like smeared glasses, creeping under the wet wallpaper, sentences rolling on, the face under uncombed brown hair patches of red on the sides, eyes under crooked tight eyebrows, plucked, nineteen-twenties pencil eyebrows on a fat forehead, bumps and furrow of flesh...

"...a husband at all, more like a juvenile delinquent, yeah, juvenile delinquent age forty-seven down in the..."

...the door quietly behind him, and came closer, not saying anything but with a sad sad look on his face looking at me, at them...

Fat mouth moving, coming closer, pale mottle skin of face leaning over her now, mouth moving, words under dirty layer of plastic, eyes bloodshot and rimmed with yellow...

Andrea's fingers slid round the handle and the fingers fitted in the finger grooves, and then she hit with such force that she came right out of the chair. As her mother fell to the floor she nearly dragged Andrea with her, till Andrea let go of the knife handle, and she was left bending over the dying woman, staring into those eyes full of hate till the hate turned into a wide stare.

CHAPTER TWENTY-FIVE

WANTED TO KNOW why it couldn't be the way it was in the old-style novels, where a man's fate was decided on the merits of a choice he makes: up comes the moral dilemma—he makes the wrong choice and the rest of his life is misery, but if he makes the right painful choice, his spiritual rewards outweigh all his personal afflictions, and he emerges stronger in the places he has been injured. But there is always the point of choice. The world waits while he works up to his decision.

It isn't that way. Things happen to the world, that's all. They happen to the world that is inside us, each person. You can be the worst bastard in the world and wing through life untouched by any black forces, or even the knowledge of evil. You can lay your life down for your fellow man and wind up the worst villain in history.

Delsing just listened to all this with no comment, it was the kind of thing I suspect he was thinking all the time. He can't get it out, but I make my way by telling things to people. Delsing couldn't answer me. All he could do was nod, and at least I was aware that he knew.

The world is a fucking awful place. That's all.

And it turns around and comes back where it was before. That is its only design. We can come ten billion years and we are face to face with a fossil that moves its bony legs.

Andrea was back where I had first found her, down in the skid row part of town, where Vancouver began to tear the logs out of the Pacific Northwest, finally to lay concrete for dead junkies and syphilitic Indians, and the city police station. That meant the iron cot that smells of the preceding drunk's urine. She was there, and the story was in the newspapers, and I knew they had it right: she killed her mother. I knew it was right. It was the thing that had to happen. I had known something like that was going to happen, but I had thought she was after herself—I had half-braced myself for her white body in the water, clothes fanned out around her, head bumping regularly on the pier.

She came to my place before she went down to skid row. When I got home from school there was a note on my bed.

> *Don't come and visit me. I will write if they let me,*
> *and if I want to. Just go to my place and take whatever*
> *you want and give the rest to my brother.*

I didn't have any idea what was going on. Come and visit her where? I thought of going to all the beaches in Vancouver, all the quiet ones away from the water where people went. But that wasn't right. Probably the turret was the only place I could find out anything. I didn't want to go. I wanted to slip away, into some other world where there wasn't any Andrea. If I had never met her outside the city jail she would not have existed, she could have been one of the anonymous white-faced girls in the coffee clubs. What did I want at her place? There was her mother, with relatives—they wouldn't know where she lived. But it sounded as if she wanted me to go there. There must be something there I was supposed to find.

So I drove down. I saw it in the afternoon *Sun* on the corner newsstand: BEATNIK GIRL SLAYS MOTHER.

I wanted to be in Europe, in a circle of buildings and people who never heard of Vancouver. I stopped the car and read the paper in a back alley off Davie Street. I was staring at the paper, some tire advertisement, when a big truck honked at me. Now I was scared.

I turned round and started east, toward that end of town, driving carefully still in the rain. I wasn't flying to her. I drove down bright Granville Street of theatre lights, bulbs going round and round, till Hastings Street, and turned right into its dreary canyon of slanting rain, east, stopping for the red lights, the little windshield wipers rubbing back and forth leaving streaks. The newspaper was hanging off the front of the seat beside me, headlines hanging down. The traffic thinned out, and I arrived at Main Street. I drove quickly around into the alley behind the police station, and parked in the dark rainy lot among black police cars, their wet roofs gleaming in rows off into the dark.

This was the place I remembered...how fast it was they dragged me out of the police truck and across the lot, to a door in a cement wall with a bulb over it, finally the elevator that came and whisked us silently to the room with the long counter. And now I walked around to the front, pulling my coat collar up and hunching over the way you learn in the persistent Vancouver rain.

Outside the two little court rooms three men sat on the yellow wooden bench, witnesses or defendants, smoking nervous cigarettes. I looked at them and they looked back. We all wanted something to take us away somewhere, out of this. I walked up to the desk where a girl in a blue serge suit sat and waited.

"I've come to see the girl in the newspapers. Andrea Harrison," I said.

"Are you a relative?" she said, automatically pulling a writing pad in front of her.

"No."

She looked blankly at my face, somewhere above my eyes.

She was waiting for me to say something more. Then she was going to say something.

"I'm her fiancé," I said.

But I had to say something. I couldn't say I was her ex-lover. I said fiancé, a word I had never used before in my life except in jokes.

The woman was looking in a long black book with lined pages between hard black covers. She was poking her pencil into the edges of her tightly rolled hair. Her finger came to rest on a line. There was no long fingernail, just the manicured end of the finger. There was rain on my forehead. I wiped at it with the back of my hand. There was rain on my glasses, too.

"She isn't here. She went to Crease Clinic this afternoon."

It was the mental hospital. Part of it was for the city police. I said thank you and walked out of the building. There were no matches in the car to light a cigarette.

I drove back, then, back downtown, to the West End. The rain did that thing it does in the late afternoon, it picked up weight, came down hard in big drops. The traffic wheels beside me splashed through water, and the windshield wipers went back and forth, sweeping water off the glass.

At her place I got out of the car and pulled my coat up over my head and ran around to the fire escape, up to the door. I knocked hard and waited. Leonard came to the door with a magazine in his hand and his hair messed up.

"Hi," I said.

"Hi."

He stepped back and I went in, stamping my feet and letting my coat back on my shoulders.

"I got a note to come here and fix things up," I said.

He gestured at the stairs, and went back to the kitchen where the stove was.

I went up the stairs, taking a right turn every six steps, up into the turret, into her room, a circle of windows. In the middle of the bare wooden floor was a candle stuck with its own wax, and a window was open—the wind must have blown out the flame, how long ago? There were books all around, lying open on their faces, crumpled in corners. A pile of books held the window open. The bed was made up, but wrinkled, and there were clothes on it, a small brassiere. I walked over and held it up. It was small, I could see her putting it on, awkward elbows in the air. But from the back, I couldn't see her face. In my mind I tried to turn her around—she kept her face from me. I couldn't remember much about her face.

I sat down on the bed, scene of earlier love, remembering the night we first lay there together when I didn't go home, lying there with our hands together. The light ran along the edge of her from below her breasts to the rise of her thighs. That light was like her name, Andrea. I thought about all the other nights when she was here alone. This round room with Andrea in the middle, the bed, behind the glass that held out the world. There was a picture from a magazine stuck to the wood between two windows, a Chagall print in blue and green and red, two lovers embracing at the bottom, a giant rooster in the sky above them, and they were looking up at it from their holding of each other. You could see that as soon as you opened your eyes in the morning.

I got up slowly, and walked over to the window, wondering what I was going to do, and wondering if I was going to do anything. I pulled back the cotton cloth and looked out at the rain. It was almost over now, and I could see the shining roof of my yellow car.

It was from here that someone had looked out that morning when I was sitting on the grass watching all night. It was probably Andrea.

But had she wanted me to find something here? There were papers lying all over the place, but I didn't find a note. There was the room, of course—she could have been asking me to see the room, something of her. She knew about my mind going away all this time. With religious intent I hadn't said I love you for a long time, as at the beginning. This room was the right symmetrical ending. If I could survive this, it was all gone. But she was still out at that place, Crease Clinic. She was tied on a table where they shot a drug into her arm, sleeve rolled up in a bunch above the elbow...

The tape recorder was on the other side of the bed. The top was off and there was a full tape on one of the reels. I squatted down and attached the end of the tape to the other reel. I was surprised for the moment by my calm fingers. I turned the machine on and sat on the bed, waiting. If this was her way of telling me the things she found hard to say, it would be here now. I listened.

There was nothing. But I kept listening, waiting. The early darkness of a rainy day was coming down around the windows, through the cotton curtains. It got completely dark, and the tape came to an end. The loose end slapped around for a while, before I leaned over and turned it off.

I stood up and looked around. I thought somebody would take care of all this—her uncle. Did she have an uncle? He would get everything together and do something with it. He would pack the little brassiere with everything else.

Downstairs I walked past Leonard. He didn't try to say anything. I opened the door myself and went outside. The rain was over, and everything was shining in the streetlight. I left my coat open and walked to my car. When I opened the door my hand was wet from the handle. I drove away without wiping it dry.

I drove over the Burrard Street Bridge on the way home. There was no one walking, and the bridge was gleaming after the rain. I couldn't see the white lines on the road. Under the bridge the sea began. Out over the sky to the west heavy dark clouds, reached out to join the horizon. I thought about the sea, her sea. The sea is a jail, I thought. Then I thought how stupid that was. She was in a jail now. The sea is a jail of her mind. That was stupid too. I couldn't think of anything that wasn't stupid, so I stopped thinking. I just drove home over the shiny black streets. The neon signs over the small stores shone brighter after the rain. I didn't remember to turn off the windshield wipers till I was almost home.

Delsing was studying when I got in. I hung my wet coat in the bathroom, and made some instant coffee.

"You get any cigarettes?" asked Delsing, without looking up from his book.

"Yeah, here," I said, throwing the package on the desk in front of him.

"You were gone long enough," he said.